red handed

Also by Gena Showalter

Oh My Goth

red handed

GENA SHOWALTER

POCKET BOOKS **MTV BOOKS**

New York **London** **Toronto** **Sydney**

POCKET BOOKS, a division of Simon & Schuster, Inc.
1230 Avenue of the Americas, New York, NY 10020

First MTV Books/Pocket Books trade paperback edition June 2007

Designed by Carla Jayne Little

Manufactured in the United States of America

10   9   8   7   6   5   4

ISBN-13:   978-1-4165-3224-8
ISBN-10:   1-4165-3224-2

For information regarding special discounts for bulk purchases, please contact Simon & Schuster Special Sales at 1-800-456-6798 or business@simonandschuster.com.

To Brad Redus—an amazing friend.

To Sherry Rowland—invaluable to me.

To Cody Quine—welcome to the family!
(If possible, I would dot the "i" with a heart.)

Acknowledgments

Thank you to Jill Monroe, Sheila Fields, Donnell Epperson, and Betty Sanders for the late-night reads.

1

New Chicago
Sometime in the near future . . .

I'd always loved the night, where anything could happen and everything usually did. The forbidden . . . the unexpected . . . the *bad*. Nothing seemed real in the ethereal light of the moon. Sins were easily forgiven. Why not play? everyone thought—*I* had once thought. Why not enjoy?

At the moment, loud, gyrating music pounded through the darkness, vibrating with so much force the ground shook and the trees swayed. In the center of a forest clearing, my friends danced around a blazing fire, and in the flickering gold and shadows their hands were everywhere. Their mouths were kissing hungrily, their bodies moved to the rhythm of the rock, fast and erratic. Sexual.

Those who weren't dancing were lounging against the circling trees, drinking beer, laughing, and smoking Onadyn, or "Snow Angels," as we called the cigs—the drug of choice for humans nowadays. It was a deoxygenating drug meant only for the aliens who had invaded our planet so many years ago. A deoxygenating drug that made humans, who needed oxygen to survive, feel as if they were soaring through the heavens, untouchable and invincible (if it didn't kill them).

"I should know," I muttered under my breath.

I'd flown for years before being forced into rehab. (Twice) I'd been too wasted to recall the first, but I remembered the second very well, the memory of it burned into my brain.

My mom had picked me up after school one day. Uncaring of her reaction, I'd smoked a Snow Angel just before she arrived. Not enough to pass out, but just enough to fragment my thoughts and emotions, making me loopy, disoriented, and a total pain in the ass.

Nothing could touch me when I was like that. Not anger, not fear, not sadness.

She'd known what I'd done the instant she spotted me—the glassy eyes and blue lips always gave users away—yelling in front of the other kids waiting for their parents, "Damn you, Phoenix! Is this how you put your life back together?"

Some of the kids around me snickered; some stared at me with disgust. Still uncaring, I didn't sit up, just continued to lounge on the steps. The sun was shining, bright and warm. Maybe I'd spend the rest of the day here.

"I asked you a question, young lady."

"And I didn't give you an answer," I'd replied with a laugh. "Now hush."

"Hush? Hush! You're ruining your life, you're ruining *my* life, and you don't even care!" She abandoned the car and stomped to me, scowling down at me. "I'm supposed to go to work, but I can't leave you alone like this. No telling what you'll do."

I laughed again. "You're a waitress. It's not like you make a difference in the world. And you know what else? Whatever I do is my business, not yours."

Hurt washed over her face, but she squared her chin. "Whether I make a difference or not, my job is what pays for your food and your shelter and your clothes." She grabbed my shoulders and shook me. "Your actions become my business when you steal my hard-earned money to buy the very drugs that are killing you. Your actions become my business when you run away to God knows where and I don't see you for days."

"Just, I don't know, shut up and go away or something. You're ruining my buzz." Dizzy, I tried to push her hands away but didn't have the strength. That, too, made me laugh.

She didn't reply for several strangled seconds, just stared at me as if I were a bottle of poison and she'd just digested the entire contents. Other parents had arrived, I realized, and watched us unabashedly.

My mom realized it, too, and wheeled around to face

them. "What are you staring at?" she snapped. "Get your kids and go home."

"Your daughter is seriously disturbed," someone muttered.

"She's a menace," someone else, a man, said. "And if she ever comes near my child, I'll call the cops and have her locked away."

"Don't worry, Daddy," one of the more popular girls at the school said in a snotty voice. I couldn't recall her name, but I knew she was a straight-A student, an all-around goody-goody, and someone I despised because she always seemed so put together, as if the world were her own personal treasure chest. "I'd rather kill myself than go near her."

I pushed to my feet, wobbling as another wave of dizziness struck. I meant to approach her, realized I'd fall, so remained in place, saying instead, "You can fuck the hell off." With that, I gave her and her dad a double-birded salute. "Feel free to kill yourself like you promised. Or maybe call me and I'll come over and do it for you."

There was a gasp. An enraged snarl.

My mom dragged me into the car after that. I hadn't cared at the time, but she'd cried the entire way home and shipped me to rehab that very evening.

Once I'd sobered up, the memory had embarrassed and shamed me. Still did. I'd made my own mother feel worthless, and I'd laughed about it.

I didn't want to be that uncaring girl ever again. I kept thinking, *What if, next time I use, I do something worse?* What if, next time, I couldn't be forgiven—by my mom or myself? I mean, a guy I met in rehab had later killed himself because he'd been humiliated by the things he'd done to support his habit.

I hadn't reached that point. *And I won't.*

I refused to fly anymore. Which was hard, now that I was back in school and surrounded by friends who flew every weekend. Harder still as I stood in that ethereal moonlight, the world around me beckoning with promises of numbness and invincibility.

Those promises had always been my downfall.

I just, I didn't fit in with the other kids at school. They saw me as the goody-goody had. Worthless, untrustworthy. Tainted. These were the only kids that accepted and understood me, so I didn't want to leave them.

Stay strong, Phoenix. Stay strong. As I sipped my beer, I leaned against the jagged bark of a tree. I'd arrived only a few minutes ago, parked in front of an abandoned warehouse like everyone else, and trekked through the forest. Late. As always. I had debated coming at all.

Now, as I studied the scene in front of me, I realized I shouldn't have come, no matter how much I missed my friends. No matter how alone I felt.

No matter how determined I thought my resolve to remain sober.

Plumes of white smoke wafted, like mist, almost like ghosts, enveloping the kids who were puffing Snow Angels. I bit my bottom lip. Oh, the temptation . . . months ago I would have joined them without thought. Would have inhaled the sweet, after-rain scent of the drug and soared through the stars.

A painful need to do just that washed through me. In seconds I could be giddy, invincible. *Fly . . . fly . . .* I could forget the way my dad had walked out on me and my mom two years ago; I could forget my mom's constant disappointment in me. I could even forget the little stresses of the day, where it didn't matter who liked me and who didn't.

"Phoenix!" a familiar voice called happily. "Thank God. You came, you sexy bitch."

I glanced to my left, following the direction of the words. My friend, Jamie Welsh, was approaching, her black curls bouncing on her shoulders. She smiled, her expression as happy as her tone. The firelight flickered over her heavily painted face and illuminated her black syn-leather dress and knee-high boots.

"I couldn't stay away," I admitted.

Jamie threw her arm around my shoulders and clinked our beers together. "You left Chateau Insano two weeks ago, but this is the first I've seen you outside of class. What's that about?"

Chateau Insano. Our name for rehab. It fit. I *had* gone crazy for a while, hitting the walls, screaming, destroying any piece of furniture—or person—I could get my hands on, all in an attempt to fight my way free.

"My mom's become my warden," I said, the words dripping with self-deprecation. "I spend most of my time at home now."

"Poor baby," she said, sympathetic. "Thank God you escaped tonight, though." She drained the rest of her beer and tossed the glass onto the ground. "It's gonna get freaky!"

I tapped my foot to the beat of the music, trying to cut off a groan. "Something going down?"

"Just the usual. You know, all the things our parents hate. As if they didn't do the same things when they were young."

I couldn't picture my mom doing anything wild, not now, not ever. She was so . . . starched. Not just her appearance: unwrinkled clothing and pale, slicked-back hair. But her personality. If she wasn't working, she was cleaning the house, not giving a single speck of dust time to settle. She never drank, never seemed to have a moment of relaxation.

Pacing, worrying, *those* were her favorite pastimes. *Because of me,* I thought, a little sad.

"Hey," Jamie said, drawing my attention. "You're all stiff. You, like, need to lighten up. Have you seen Allison Stone's brother? That'll help you for sure."

"No." I hadn't even known Allison had a brother. In fact, I'd thought Allison had moved away a year ago. "Allison's here?"

"Yeah, but forget Allison. Allison Smallison, we want to talk about her brother. He graduated a few years ago, before you moved here, then joined the military. The few, the proud, or some other shit," she said, rolling her eyes. "I don't think you two ever met."

"We didn't."

"You'll hate yourself for that when you see him." As she spoke, Jamie withdrew a small, plastic vial from the hidden, zippered pouch on the side of her boot. Druggies always had ways to hide their stash. "I've kept an eye out for him all these years, but he rarely comes home. Until now," she added with a wicked smile. "He's finally here."

I almost groaned again when I spotted the vial. Onadyn, or "Breathless," the liquid form of the drug. Stronger than powder, more potent than pills. Ten thousand times better than Snow Angels. You didn't just fly to the stars with Breathless, you *became* one.

For a little while, at least, I reminded myself, but I was unable to tear my gaze from the vial. My hand shook with the desire to reach out and snatch it. I could drain it before Jamie even realized what I'd done.

When you crash, you crash hard, Phoenix. You don't need that right now. After Breathless, a person burned and ached and dreamed of their next hit. They would kill for it. Steal for it.

But it's so damn good. One more time couldn't possibly hurt me.

Jamie uncorked the top. She drained half and offered the rest to me. I continued to stare at the clear, swirling liquid for a moment, hungry, so hungry. Tremors raked me. *I'll end up back in rehab. I'll hurt my mom again. Everything I've gained will be lost.*

"Want a sip?" she asked.

Finally, I gathered my wits and shook my head. "No thanks."

She frowned and pushed the bottle closer to me, right under my nose. "Your mom won't know."

I experienced a flicker of irritation—and need. She was right. Mom would never have to know. I could—I ground my teeth together. *No. Stop!* I wasn't like that. Not anymore. "No thanks," I repeated firmly.

Undeterred, she waved the bottle back and forth. The clear liquid swished back and forth, nearly hypnotizing me. For some, Onadyn held a faint dewy scent. For others, for most actually, it was scentless. How I wished it was scentless to me. My mouth watered.

"You absolutely positively sure?" she asked.

No. "Yes." I turned my face away.

Jamie shrugged and downed the rest.

I released a sigh of . . . relief, I hope.

The vial joined the beer bottle on the ground, and they rolled together. Damn. I looked again. "You have *got* to see him," Jamie said.

My brows furrowed in confusion. "Who?"

"Ryan Stone, silly. Allison's brother. Why he came, I don't know and I don't care. I'm just glad he's here." Her face scrunched. "I don't know why his sister came, either. Her, I do care about. I wish she'd have stayed home, the snobby bitch."

Allison had never partied with us. She'd been one of those

goody-goodies who made life appear easy. She'd practically floated down the halls, a golden halo on her head, angel wings on her back. Everyone (but us) had loved her.

"Remember how she used to glare at us with disgust during class?" Jamie asked. "I wanted to scratch her eyes out."

Yeah, I remembered. I'd been happy to see her leave. "Tell me again what's so special about Ryan. With a sister like his, he can't be all that great."

Jamie giggled, her voice a little hoarse and a lot shallow as her oxygen levels dropped. "Wait till you see him. He's beyond doable. He's—" She looked past the bonfire and frowned. "Where'd he go? If he's making out with—wait. There," she said, pointing. "Yum yum."

My gaze followed the direction of her finger, but I only saw kids I knew. A few were still standing. Most were collapsed on the ground, strung out and staring up at the black velvet sky, flying high. "I don't see him."

Jamie stumbled forward, chuckled, and righted herself. She latched onto my wrist, tugging me close. "Look *there*."

Curiosity intensifying, I searched again—and this time, I saw him. I knew it was him and didn't need it confirmed. Dear God. My mouth fell open and warm tingles immediately spread over my skin. He had brown hair, yet there appeared to be strands of gold in the firelight. And even from the distance, I could see that his eyes were bright blue, crystalline, more breathtaking than Onadyn.

His sharp cheekbones gave him a menacing appearance, as

if he wanted to fight the entire world. He had a slightly crooked nose, as if the world had taken him up on the offer a time or two. He also had the faintest dusting of a shadow beard on his jaw. Very . . . older man meets preppy. Not like the boys at my school, who were still in the early stages of muscledom (not that they'd ever admit it).

Ryan wasn't just hot; he was blazing.

Obviously more experienced than the high school crowd surrounding him, he radiated an I'll-kick-your-ass-if-you-talk-to-me vibe. He wasn't drinking or smoking, just watching everything that happened around him.

"Killer, isn't he?" Jamie asked with another wicked grin. Then she wobbled on her feet and frowned. "Stupid shoes."

Yeah, it's your shoes and not the lack of oxygen in your brain, I thought dryly, still not taking my gaze from Ryan.

He chose that moment to glance over at me, as if he'd sensed my scrutiny. For a split second, our eyes clashed together, locked. A shiver traveled the length of my spine just before he looked away, dismissing me as he would a pesky fly.

Irritation flooded me, and my jaw hardened. Boys—younger, older, didn't matter—always did that. Looked away. I was cute, or so I'd been told, but I wasn't beautiful like Jamie and so I was, apparently, unworthy of prolonged attention. I wasn't overflowing in the breast department, either. Another strike against me.

"He's an asshole," I gritted out.

Jamie muttered something unintelligible and stumbled

forward once more. Reaching out, I wound my arm around her waist. "Come on," I said. "Time to lie down."

"Nightie-night then?"

"Definitely."

Her only response was a strangled gasp.

I eased her onto the dirt and grass, dropping my beer along the way. Jamie was heavier than she appeared and her dress didn't bend easily. When I finally got her settled on the ground, I righted her clothing to cover all the important parts.

Crouching beside her, I peered down and sighed. Her green eyes were glassy and fixed straight ahead. Her lips were parted and tinted blue as her lungs tried unsuccessfully to suck in air. Was this what my mother had seen, each time she'd looked at me?

There was nothing else I could do for Jamie. She'd fly for the rest of the night.

With another sigh, I pushed to my feet. I turned toward the dancing circle, not knowing what to do with myself just then. Stay guard over Jamie in case someone decided to molest her? Go home before my mom found out I'd left?

Nah. I couldn't leave Jamie. I'd never forgive myself if something happened to her.

Unbidden, my gaze slid back to Ryan. He was watching me, I realized with surprise. And pleasure. I'd never met a boy who radiated such *power*.

Again, warm tingles fluttered over my skin. My stomach

clenched. I hated the way I was reacting to him. That had never happened to me before.

Before he could look away from me, *I* looked away from *him*. Ha! *How do you like that?*

The music reached a high-pitched crescendo, echoing through the night. In less than an hour, everyone here would be passed out. There was too much smoke in the air for anyone to remain sober for long—even me. So as soon as everyone had nodded off, I'd head home. No one could hurt Jamie if *everyone* was snoozing.

But I hated the thought of going home as much as I hated the thought of staying here for much longer. I'd have to deal with my mom. I shuddered. Things weren't smooth between us yet. She was constantly going through my things, looking for drugs. She wasn't even close to trusting me.

Why should she? I snuck out at the first opportunity. I'd just, well, I'd really needed a break from her sad, you'll-be-back-on-drugs-soon-enough glances. I'd needed to forget.

Don't think about that. Not here of all places, where temptation lurks. What could I do to keep my mind occupied? Dance?

No. If I joined the dancing circle, the fire would heat me inside and out and my resolve would weaken. I would smoke. If I smoked, I wouldn't stop until I was numb. And if I became numb, I wouldn't care about staying sober.

In that moment, I felt more out of place than I had in a long time. I didn't belong here, and I didn't belong with the other kids at school, the ones who considered me better off dead. I didn't belong at home with my mother, either, a woman who made me feel guilty and depressed every time I looked at her.

"Take your friend and go home," a deep male voice suddenly said.

Startled, I whipped my attention to the side. My eyes widened. Ryan Stone was standing next to me, a slash of black clothes and intimidating male. I hadn't even heard him approach. Not the snap of a twig, not the roll of a rock or the pound of a boot.

Up close, he towered over my five-foot-seven frame. His shoulders were broad, his arms hard and strong. His eyes were . . . freaky. I'd thought they were pretty from a distance. Wrong. They practically swirled with blue and flecks of purple. They didn't look like human eyes.

Was he an alien?

No, couldn't be. Except for his eyes, he appeared to be fully human. Aliens did not. I'd always thought they were recognizable with one glance. The Delenseans had blue skin and multiple arms. The Bre-Alees excreted slime, so they always appeared wet. The Mecs changed colors with their moods, glowing like neon signs. The Arcadians had similar bodies and facial features to us but their skin was much paler and their eyes were a metallic purple color, inhuman.

There were more alien types than I could name. Still. Same story. They looked different from us. *The ones I know about, at least*. . . . But I did not want to consider *that*.

Ryan frowned at me, and it was one of the darkest expressions I'd ever seen. Scary.

"Take your friend and go home," he repeated.

"Why?" I asked, raising my chin, refusing to budge. He'd dismissed me only a few minutes ago. The fact that he was now eager to get rid of me only made it worse. Who did he think he was?

"There's going to be trouble with the Outers tonight, and you do *not* want to be a part of it."

Aliens a.k.a. "the Outers." I had nothing against them; they'd lived and walked among us for over seventy years. I'd learned in history class that they'd only been allowed into our school system and workforce about twenty years ago. But they'd always been a part of my life and had never caused me trouble, so Ryan could go screw himself.

Outers rarely caused trouble, to be honest; they were too afraid of being killed by A.I.R., Alien Investigation and Removal, an elite unit very similar to police or military or FBI. Except deadlier. Meaner. More blood thirsty.

They were the stuff of legends and movies.

Everyone, even humans, feared them. They could mow you down like roadkill if they even suspected you were guilty of helping an alien commit a violent crime. And it would be perfectly legal. They were judge, jury, and executioner.

"What makes you think there'll be trouble?" I asked, humoring him. A part of me didn't want him to leave my side.

He didn't look at me when he said, "Maybe I spotted a few aliens when I hiked through the forest."

"So," I said with a laugh.

"So," he said with a scowl.

I snorted and waved a hand in dismissal. "Are you an Outer hater or something?"

Ryan's eyes narrowed, but he didn't answer.

"You paranoid, then?" I'd been thinking about leaving only a few minutes ago. Now I wanted to stay. Maybe it was the rebel in me. Maybe it was the fact that I was talking to one of the hottest boys I'd ever seen—a boy who, with only a few words, had made me feel more alive than I had in a long, long time, even though he couldn't wait to get rid of me. "Think the Outers are out to get us and steal our planet? Well, guess what? You should have paid better attention in class. Even I know the War of the Species is over. Has been for like sixty years. Everyone's friendly now."

To end the war that had almost destroyed our planet, the Outers and humans had signed a peace treaty, which gave aliens permission to stay here and A.I.R. the right to police and destroy as needed. I'd had to memorize the stupid thing, not that I could recall a single word now.

A muscle ticked under Ryan's eye. "You know for a fact that they're friendly?"

"When was the last reported violent crime, hmm?"

"So the media reports everything now? That's a newsflash

to me." He laughed, but the sound lacked humor. "Ignorant, that's what you are. You have no idea what you're messing with, little girl."

Ignorant? Little girl? My eyes narrowed, just like his had done earlier. I closed some of the distance between us. He smelled like firelight and pine. "Every girl here is my age or younger. What'd you come here for? To get you a piece of ass from one of these *little girls*, right? So what does that make you?"

His jaw hardened, making it a determined square. "That's not—"

A strange, eerie howl suddenly cut through the night. The sound was raspy, animalistic. Close. Startled, I glanced left and right, halfway expecting a wolf to be nearby. Not that there were many left in the world.

Just my luck, though, the last one still kicking would be nearby, hungry for a big, delicious platter of human girl.

Ryan cursed under his breath. He withdrew a weird-looking gun from his side, and I gasped. I backed away, palms up, the wolf forgotten. "What are you doing? Put that away before someone gets hurt."

Another howl rent the air, followed by another and yet another. Obviously, there wasn't just one wolf. There were . . . God knows how many. I shuddered.

"I told you to leave," Ryan said. Frowning, he twisted a dial on the side of the gun. "But no, you had to stay. That decision's going to cost you."

The howls blended with multiple growls, all of them low and menacing.

I lost my focus on Ryan's weapon, forgot about his threat. "What *is* that?" I whispered, trying to see past the trees to something, anything, that could be making such a terrible sound.

"That's death," Ryan said bleakly. "And it's too late to avoid it now."

2

Within the blink of an eye, a horde of animal-like creatures burst through the far coppice of trees, green leaves trembling against their onslaught. The creatures were flesh colored with not a single strand of hair on their wrinkled skin. They crawled on all fours. No, not true, I realized. They bounded, jumping from ground to tree stump, stump to ground.

I gaped at the sight of them, repulsed and frightened, but unable to look away. Morbid fascination held me in its tight grasp. Kids screamed and ran around the fire and through the thicket, panicked, trying to get away. My heart began an erratic drumbeat in my chest, a rushed *da da da*. I'd seen some weird-looking Outers over the years, but I'd never seen anything like these.

My eyes widened as one of the creatures jumped on top of an unconscious boy, meshing its mouth over the boy's and—

"Oh my God," I gasped out.

White-gold pinpricks of light flashed through the air between them, and the boy's body shook, as if something was being pulled from deep within him. He was unconscious, but still he struggled, still he flailed.

"I don't think so," I heard Ryan say. He aimed his strange gun and fired once, twice. Pretty blue beams lit up the night. I could feel their heat, even from where I stood.

More human screams blared, but the light from the gun didn't touch any of them. No, the beams slammed into the monsters, freezing them in place.

Those who escaped the blasts chased and jumped on top of the panicked humans, knocking them to the ground, attempting to . . . kiss them? They lowered their mouths, opening wide, fusing alien and human together.

"Wh—what are those?" I gasped out.

"Sybilins," Ryan spat, firing again. Another stream of blue flashed. This one hit a monster dead center in the back and it, too, froze. But there were so many of them, and their numbers only seemed to grow with every second that passed.

Sybilins? I'd never heard the word before. I'd never *dealt* with anything like this before, and I wasn't sure what to do. But I didn't even consider running. My friends were here, some of them helpless, flying. Like Jamie, still at my feet. I could not abandon them simply to save myself.

Several of the creatures—God, how many of them were out here?—growled and howled with rage, focusing their attention on Ryan. And me. Their eyes glowed red, bright red, perhaps the exact shade of radioactive blood.

"Run," Ryan commanded without looking my way. "Go to you car. I'll hold them off." He fired his gun with one hand and withdrew a knife from a hidden sheath at his waist with the other.

The sheer menace of him was as startling as the Outers' appearance. "Like hell," I said. I bent down and grabbed two rocks. Straightening, I bounced the heavy weights in my hands, preparing to throw them, to fight.

"Leave!" Ryan barked. "This isn't a game."

"Really?" I said dryly. I couldn't help it. I faced the aliens, adding, "You mean I don't get a prize if I'm still alive in the morning?"

Ryan cast me a dark glare and I could tell he wanted to shake me. Or kill me himself. But he turned back to the creatures, feet planted on the ground as he fired several more rounds. "Things are about to get ugly."

"I kind of had a suspicion," I replied, gripping the rocks more tightly. The fear hadn't left me, and only seemed to grow.

"You can still run."

Running and hiding sounded good. But I couldn't. I wouldn't. That would make me a coward. That would make me no better than my dad, who had abandoned me and Mom when things got tough.

I'd hated him for that. I wouldn't turn around and do the same thing.

Ryan's gun held the monsters off for a bit, but soon they learned how to dodge the hot, blue streams and leapt toward us, closing in. Almost . . . there . . . bile rose in my throat, but I managed to hold steady.

As Ryan fired, I launched a rock. The gray stone slammed into a wrinkled face, right between glowing red eyes. My rock didn't stop or even slow the creature down, but only enraged it further. Fear continued to stab at me, sharper than a knife.

The creature snarled low in its throat and flashed a funnel-like tongue at me. It was so close now, I could see the yellow saliva dripping from its too-large mouth.

Again Ryan fired, but the beast bounded left, then right, reaching me in the next second and knocking me to the ground. I still had one rock left and used it to smash the monster in the temple.

Howling, it rolled off me. Ryan used its distraction to his advantage and shot it in the face. It froze, posed exactly as it had been, features contorted in pain, that disgusting yellow saliva half dripping from its chin.

"Thanks," I muttered, pushing myself into a crouch. I couldn't stand on my own. My arms and legs were too shaky. It had touched me; that *thing* had touched me, and I felt violated. Enraged and sick.

Expression bleak, Ryan offered me a helping hand. I took it, and his strong fingers closed around me. My shaking grew worse as he hauled me to my feet. "Good work with the rock."

"Thanks," I repeated. More human screams—terrified,

pain-filled—pierced the darkness. Goose bumps broke over my skin. "What's happening?"

Ryan kept one arm extended, firing in a quick half circle, protecting us from invasion for several precious seconds. "The Sybilins are sucking the water out of your friends, drying them out."

His words echoed in my mind, surreal, almost foreign. How was that possible?

How is any *of this possible?* I thought, incredulous. Sucking the water out of human bodies . . . I'm not sure I would have believed it if I'd seen it in a movie or read it in a book.

Aliens were nonviolent, working and going to school side-by-side with humans. *Like* humans. Right?

Not these Sybilins, that's for sure.

"Where did they come from?" I managed, hand covering my throat.

"Does it matter?" Ryan returned, dialing his weapon to a hotter setting. I knew it was hotter because I could feel the singe of it, nearly blistering my skin. "Shit!" he gritted out. "This isn't working. They're still multiplying."

Without another word, he raced forward. When the creatures—the Sybilins—came within striking distance, he cut them with his knife. Yellow liquid spewed from them, thicker than their saliva, dripping on the ground. Ugh. There was a human girl out there fighting, as well, I noticed.

Allison Stone, I realized a moment later.

For a moment, I just watched, awed and terrified. Ryan

and his sister fought the Outers expertly, slashing with their hands, feet light and quick. The motions were almost a dance. Lethal, controlled, bloody.

Obviously, they'd done this before. Perhaps many times before. I'd been in a few fights myself, but nothing had ever been this violent. Nothing had ever been so in-your-face fatal.

I had to help them.

I bent down, afraid to switch my focus as I searched for more rocks. I felt only dirt.

Two hysterical kids raced past me, knocking me onto my ass in their haste to escape. As I struggled to right myself, one of the kids tripped over Jamie's body, scrambled upright, then continued running. Jamie gave no reaction.

I should follow them, I thought; I knew I should, despite my desire to protect.

Instead, I found myself finding and grabbing onto a long, thick branch. It was bare and jagged. Perfect. I was unprepared for the macabre scene unfolding, yes, but I would go down with a fight.

I stepped toward the circle and stopped, a thought shooting through my mind. Would I be a distraction to Ryan and Allison?

They knew what they were doing. I didn't. If I hindered them or caused them to be harmed, everyone here would be doomed. "Think, think," I chanted under my breath, my grip tightening on the stick. I moved forward another step, then stopped again. *What damage can I really do with a stick?*

"Two on your left," I heard Ryan say.

I spun, but there was no one to my left. All of the monsters were now in the center, battling Ryan and his sister. He must have been talking to Allison. I whipped back to the fire just in time to see Allison pivot, a blur of black as she fired off two quick shots, nailing both of her targets in their chests.

They didn't freeze; they burned to ash. Flesh sizzled, soot filled the air, nearly choking me.

What should I do? What would most help them?

"We need backup," Allison grunted, swinging up her leg and bringing it down with intense force. The blow slammed into a creature's back, forcing it onto its stomach. She fired; it too died a burning, flaming death, its screams echoing in my ears.

My mouth dried.

"They should be here soon," Ryan said.

When I saw one of the injured Sybilins crawl on top of a prone human female, I finally pulled myself from petrifaction and leapt into action. *I'll make my mother proud. I'll do whatever I have to do to protect my friends.* Ryan and Allison couldn't destroy all of the creatures, especially the ones slinking and sneaking along the dirt floor. Those *I* could handle without hindering the siblings.

As the creature's lips descended on the girl's, I closed the rest of the distance and swung my stick. Contact. My arms shook from the force as the wood smashed into its cheek and sent it tumbling to the ground.

A shocking wave of satisfaction washed through me.

"Ryan!" Allison shouted, a desperate edge to her voice. "I don't know how much longer I can keep this up."

"Just keep firing," he told her. "That's our only hope until the others get here."

I faced them and could see that Ryan and Allison were completely surrounded, still pinned in a menacing circle. The sound of grunting and groaning filled my ears. Blue and yellow lights flashed.

Okay. Taking out the Sybilins on the fringes wasn't going to do much good, I realized. I'd have to do more.

I raced forward to guard Ryan's back, but I was knocked to the ground by an Outer before I'd taken three steps. I lost my breath. Dizziness pushed through my mind, hard, and all I could do was remain in place, trying to regain my bearings.

A second later, I was flipped onto my back. One of the creatures pinned my shoulders and trapped my hands between our bodies. It fit its lips over mine. They were wet and warm, too wet, too warm, and only growing more so. I heard a *slurp*, a *pop*, then felt a hard suction pry my mouth open. That funnel-like tongue I'd seen earlier lowered over my tongue and covered the back of my throat.

I gagged.

The Sybilin began sucking, sucking. Sucking. Over and over, again and again. I couldn't breath, but that didn't panic me. I'd flown so many times I was used to going without air. What bothered me was how dry my mouth suddenly felt, how slow my blood began pumping. How tight and hard my skin became.

Fight, Phoenix. Fight! I thrashed my head, jerked on its hold, trying to dislodge it. Finally I managed to work my hands free and beat against its head. Nothing budged it. Then the creature recaptured my wrists, holding them at my sides. Not once did it stop sucking from me, draining every drop of water it could. I began to grow cold. So cold, despite the heat radiating from the still-raging bonfire beside me.

That's when panic threatened to consume me. *Stop. Stop!* I tried to scream. *Let me go!* I wasn't ready to die. I'd just gotten clean. *Stop!*

Calm down, Phoenix, I told myself in the next instant. *Calm down and think.* I forced myself to be still. What should I do? How could I get the water-stealing bastard off of me? *Better hurry . . .*

Black spots winked in and out of my vision, a spiderweb that was thickening, spreading. Time was running out, I knew that much. I really would be drained soon. My fingers were already blocks of ice, my arms almost too heavy to lift. And still the creature sucked. My entire body jerked. Spasmed.

The creature's eyes pulsed that eerie red, overshadowing even the spiderweb in my mind, becoming my only focus. Becoming . . . lethal. *Fight it. Fight this. I'm smart. I can escape.* I'd been held down like this in rehab, strapped down as I fought for freedom, for drugs. I'd been overpowered, like now, yet I had managed to escape time and time again.

Now my life hung in the balance.

Drawing deep on a reservoir of strength that always managed to surprise me, I bucked upward, the action painful, almost impossible, shaking the Sybilin to the side. It released my left wrist to steady itself. With a roar, I shoved two fingers into its eyes. I cringed at the wet warmth I encountered.

It screeched an unholy sound and rolled away from me as if I were poison, rubbing at its eyes. As it flailed, I lay still for several seconds—maybe years, maybe an eternity—trying to catch my breath, find energy. My throat hurt. Badly. My skin was like a rubber band, dry, taut, ready to snap.

Come on, come on. No time to rest. I'm making my mother proud, remember?

I lumbered to my feet. The Sybilin continued to writhe. I was afraid to touch it again, afraid it would somehow be able to attach itself to me a second time, but I approached it anyway and crouched above it. I began punching. And punching. And punching. It had tried to kill me, *would* kill me if I let it.

I didn't stop punching, even when it tried to crawl away from me. Even when it bucked and screeched, I still punched. Punched until the murdering creature ceased all movement. None of the other Sybilins came to its rescue.

Only when I stopped did I realize that my knuckles throbbed in sync with my rage. I hurt everywhere. I couldn't stop panting.

Ryan was suddenly at my side. He grabbed my upper arm and pulled me into the very spot I'd been standing before all of this began. My knees collapsed, my adrenaline rush dissipating. I fell to my butt and leaned my head against one of the trees. In that moment, I wanted to vomit. I had nothing left inside me, however, no energy to move.

"You okay?" he asked, crouching just in front of me.

"I'm . . . fine . . ." I said as my eyelids closed of their own accord. My throat was dry, raw, each word ripped from me. I'd never felt so weak in my life.

"I'm sorry I didn't get to you sooner." He tilted my chin and used his fingers to raise my eyelids and study my eyes. "I've never seen an untrained human successfully fight off a Sybilin who had already begun to feed." There was disbelief in his tone, as if seeing it still hadn't convinced him. "I don't think you'll have any permanent damage. You just need water. A lot of water."

"What about . . . the other monsters?" I couldn't suck air in fast enough.

"We've got them contained. Finally." He withdrew a canteen from one of his pant pockets and held it to my lips. "Drink."

I drank greedily, my cottony mouth absorbing every drop of moisture.

"Everything's going to be okay."

"Who . . . are . . . you?" I panted when there was nothing left. A normal boy could not have fought like that. A normal boy did not carry an arsenal to a kegger. "Who are . . . you really?"

"I'm nobody." Expression grim, he twisted and surveyed the glen.

I looked past him to do the same. Kids were strewn about, unconscious. Many of the Sybilins were still frozen in place. I gulped. "Are they dead?"

"Your friends or the Sybilins?"

"Both."

"Some of the humans will need a few days on an IV, but survival rate should be good. The Sybilins, well, some of them are alive now but they won't be for long." He said it with the slightest hint of glee.

"What—"

"No." He shook his head. "No more questions."

His sister was approaching, I noticed. She sheathed her weapons—a gun and a knife, exact replicas of Ryan's—at her waist and glanced at me. She had the same dark hair as Ryan, but her eyes were green whereas his were that freaky blue. He was tall, she was short. Where he was muscled, she looked soft.

Hard to believe the sweet-looking teenager had fought so lethally.

"What are we going to do about her?" she demanded, motioning to me with a tilt of her chin.

She was my age, seventeen, but she was trying to act older. In control. I wish I had the strength to challenge her. For the first time in years, I'd done something good. Something right. I didn't deserve condemnation. I deserved a medal. Maybe flowers. A certificate at the very least.

"Well," Allison demanded.

"Not what you're thinking," Ryan said firmly.

What was she thinking? I felt like I should know the answer, but my mind was foggy and I was suddenly having trouble sifting through the gloomy thickness.

"She's seen too much," Allison said through clenched teeth.

"She also helped us. Now drop it and find out what happened to our backup. They should have been here by now."

Allison opened her mouth to respond, but Ryan cut her off with a look. Just a single, dark look that caused her to press her lips together in a mutinous line. Then, of course, she flashed me a teeth-baring scowl as if everything was my fault and whipped around, flouncing away.

I was once again alone with Ryan—who I wasn't sure I liked. He was too bossy, too arrogant, too *everything*. But I knew I liked to look at him. He was a (sexy) mystery, a (beautiful) confusing puzzle.

"What's your name?" he asked me. His blue eyes were swirling, churning. Like an ocean tempest.

"Phoenix."

"Cute," he said.

"You wouldn't think so if it was your name," I grumbled.

His lips twitched into a smile. "I was talking about you, not the name. But I like that, too."

He thought I was cute? "It's stupid."

"No way."

"Every day someone compares me to a bird that burns to death."

"That bird also rises from its own ashes, stronger than ever before."

Okay. I now officially liked my name. I'd never thought of it that way, but loved the image. I *had* risen from my own ashes and was trying to make a better life for myself.

Ryan's expression changed from amused to regretful in the blink of an eye. "I'm very sorry, Phoenix," he said.

I blinked over at him in confusion. "For what?" Despite his earlier rudeness, he really had done nothing but help me.

"For this." His hand whipped out and smashed over my nose. The action was startling, unexpected. And . . . wet. Droplets trickled onto my lips and chin. A bitter scent wafted to my nose, then down my throat as I breathed, then onto my tongue as I opened my mouth.

I grabbed onto his wrist and tried to shove him away. He held tight. Weak as I was, I couldn't budge him. Strangely, I was only growing weaker. Swiftly so.

"My fingers are doused with a sleep aid," he explained calmly. "Sleep, Phoenix."

Our conversation, his praise of my name—obviously only a means of distracting me, I thought darkly. I tried to scream at him, to curse him, but only managed to suck in more of the bitter fumes. How dare he do this! How dare he . . . do . . . this . . .

Once again, I was faced with a black spiderweb. This one was stronger, more potent than the other. Alluring, beckoning me to peace. Like a drug. Sleep would be unbelievably sweet.

I was going to pass out; I knew I was.

But I fought it, fought the sweetness, just as I had fought the Sybilins. Just as I now fought Ryan. What was he planning to do with me? I wriggled and bucked and landed a blow to his right eye. My fist smacked into bone. Satisfaction flooded me.

"Damn it," he growled, but there was no real heat to the words. He tried to capture my hands with his free one. "That *hurt.*"

Good. I managed to punch him a second time before he pinned both of my wrists.

"I'm not going to harm you," he said. He sounded far away, slurred. "Stop fighting. Please. I'm doing this for your own good."

I didn't want to obey him, but the world around me was crumbling. No, not crumbling. Had crumbled. Completely. I had no solid anchor; I was floating. My head was too heavy, my shoulders weighted with bricks. My eyelids closed, practically glued together. For me, there was only darkness and a never-ending tunnel.

"How is she still fighting?" I heard Allison say. I hadn't heard her return.

"I don't know," Ryan said, and there was awe in his tone. "Sleep, Phoenix. Sleep." Warm breath tickled my ear. "Everything's going to be okay. I'll take care of it. I'll take care of *you*. Promise."

It was the last thing I heard before finally sinking into oblivion.

3

"Load her up," I heard a man say. He sounded far away yet familiar. Ryan, I realized a moment later. Mmm, Ryan. So cute. No, bastard. "Take her home, and be careful with her."

Suddenly I was floating.

"Kadar," Ryan called.

"Yeah?"

"Tell her parents . . . I don't know." Ryan paused. "I hate to tell them we're cops and we caught her using. I don't want her in trouble after everything she did."

"I won't mention the drugs, all right?" someone— Kadar?—replied. A man; a stranger to me. "I'll just tell them I found her like this and used her ID to track down her address. We'll leave it up to the parentals to decide what she did or didn't do at the party."

I should protest. I tried to open my mouth, but no sound emerged.

"Fine," Ryan said. "That'll be fine."

The fog claimed me again, and I knew only darkness.

———

"How could you, Nix? How *could* you?"

My mom's angry voice battered through the black shroud covering my mind. My body pulsed and throbbed with pain, I suddenly realized, as if I'd been in a wreck. A fight. *Something*.

My mouth was dry, so dry. My skin prickled and itched.

I'll take care of you. Promise.

The raspy male voice drifted into my consciousness. For a moment, I forgot everything but that voice. There was comfort in it. Assurance.

"Nix! Wake up. Right now."

There was my mom again, insistent and furious. What had I done wrong this time? Had I stayed out too late and missed curfew?

Everything's going to be okay.

Again, the male voice filled my head. I wanted to see the speaker. See his face, which somehow shimmered tauntingly in shadows. I moaned, trying to force myself to wake up completely.

As consciousness gradually claimed me, I smacked my dry lips together. God, I was thirsty.

"Finally," my mother grumbled. Her fingers closed

around my shoulders, and she shook me. "Come on, Nix. I'm tired of waiting." There was a tension-filled pause. "And I'm not going to do it anymore, not when you're responsible for every bit of my pain."

I cracked open my heavy eyelids. Too-bright sunlight filtered past my white curtains, causing my eyes to tear and burn. I rubbed a shaky hand over my face and scratched at my itchy cheek.

"Water," I rasped past the hard lump in my throat. Past the cotton in my mouth. "Water."

Exasperated, my mom stomped from my room, only to return a few minutes later with a glass. I drained the contents in seconds, sucking it down as if my life depended on it. Hmm, good. So good. Cold and wet and heaven on earth. When I finished, I set the cup on my nightstand.

"You ready to talk now?" she said.

"What's going on?" I asked. I was in my bedroom, lying on my bed, but the last thing I remembered was trees. And dirt. Moonlight. Yes, moonlight. In the next instant, a boy's face flashed into my mind. *The* boy's face, the one who kept speaking in my mind.

He had dark hair and blue eyes; he was tall. He was—his image disappeared. I fought to get it back, but . . . nothing. What was wrong with me?

"You got high again," Mom said, her scorn and disappointment clear. "*That's* what is going on."

"What?" I jolted upright. Dizziness hit me in sickening

waves, and several minutes passed before the sensation calmed. "I didn't get high." I knew that much for sure.

I'd gone to the party, I remembered that now. I'd stood on the edge of the glen, watching my friends dance and smoke, but I'd resisted. Yes, I *had* resisted. And then . . . what? Ryan Stone had approached me. That's right. Ryan Stone. My eyes widened as the night's events replayed through my mind in vivid color and sound.

Ryan was the one inside my head. His sister, Allison, had been in the forest with us. Outers had arrived and had tried to kill us. A fight had broken out. Guns had flashed and knives had glinted. My friends had almost died.

"I snuck out," I said, focusing on my mom. "I admit that. But that's all I'm guilty of. I swear I didn't use. Aliens attacked us. They tried to suck the water out of our bodies, but we fought them." I didn't mention that I'd almost become a victim myself.

Mom glared down at me, and I fought the urge to look away. We were mirror images of each other, Mom and I. We shared the same pale hair, the same big, brown eyes. The same freckles on our cute, pixie noses. The same thin bodies—why couldn't she have given me boobs? Looking at her was like looking at a delicate flower, easily stomped on. I sincerely hoped that was not the image people got when they looked at me.

"I did good, Mom."

"You get high and apparently think I'm so stupid I won't

figure it out. Then you lie to me about it. Fighting aliens? Please. Something like that would be all over the news."

"I'm telling the truth! I could have run, but I stayed and fought. I helped save lives. I . . . I thought you'd be proud of me."

She rubbed a hand over her face, massaging the lines of tension around her eyes and mouth. "Your skin is dry, Nix, as if you haven't been getting enough oxygen. There are circles under your eyes, and your lips are tinted blue. Classic signs of Onadyn use. I should know. I've seen them a thousand times."

"Mom—"

Tears filled her eyes. "I thought you'd quit. You promised me you would quit this time!"

"But Mom—"

"I'm so disappointed in you, I'm almost at a loss for words," she said, cutting me off again. "Did you learn nothing in rehab? Did you forget that drugs can and will kill you?"

"I learned," I insisted. "I know."

She snorted, wiping at the tears with the back of her hand. "I thought you'd wised up and finally realized you were sinking into a dark spiral of unhappiness and death." As she ranted, she paced the length of my room. She became a blur against the white walls, the metallic vanity, and the holographic photos of my friends. "I mean, God! You once threatened to help a girl kill herself."

My cheeks burned in shame.

"I'd never been so mortified and horrified in my life. And now, to find out you're using the very substance that turned you into that monster yet again . . ."

"I'm not lying to you. I didn't get high."

"Oh, really? A strange man found you and brought you home last night. You were unconscious and unresponsive. I thought I was going to have to take you to the hospital so they could give you a transfusion of oxygen-rich blood."

"A strange man brought me home?" I shook my head, clearing my thoughts. "What did he look like?" Had Ryan brought me here? He'd knocked me out, so it was entirely possible.

Thinking of the way he'd tricked me, the way he'd unmercifully rendered me unconscious, caused my anger levels to spike. My hands clenched into fists. *Why* had he done that?

"What did he look like?" I insisted.

"What does the man's appearance matter?" my mom said, suddenly hysterical. "He had dark hair and hazel eyes. Happy? He told me he'd found you passed out in the forest and read your ID to learn your address."

For some reason, that sounded familiar to me. I didn't know why, and my head hurt trying to reason it out. I did know the man who brought me home hadn't been Ryan. His eyes were freaky blue, not hazel.

"The man could have been a murderer, a rapist, or an alien," Mom said. "He could have killed you or worse, hurt you to the point you *wished* he'd killed you, and no one would have known. I would have spent years crying for you, worried about you, praying. Once again my life would have been thrown into turmoil because of *you*."

"I swear to God I'm clean!" Maybe I would hunt Ryan down. He'd been there. He knew the truth. My mom refused to believe me, but maybe she'd believe him.

"I'm so frustrated with you, Nix. The drugs are destroying us, and I can't take it anymore."

"Mom, you have to believe me!" My voice broke. I kept my gaze on her, silently begging her to trust me. Just this once. I was a different person now and wanted her to see it, to acknowledge it. "You can test . . . my oxygen levels," I finished lamely. If my water level was down, would my oxygen levels be down, too? If so, I'd appear guilty. "Mom, please."

"Changed your mind about the test, did you?" Laughing without humor, she tangled her hand in her pale hair; the sound of that humorless laughter echoed off the walls. Her shoulders sagged with dejection. "I'm sorry, Nix, but the evidence speaks for itself. I don't need to pay for a test."

My stomach knotted painfully. I'd never done anything to earn her trust, I knew that and was ashamed of it. I don't know why I'd expected it now. But for the first time in years, I *was* telling the truth.

I dropped my chin onto my chest and stared down at my

hands, twisting grooves into my comforter. Purple and blue branched from my knuckles to my wrists. They were so swollen, each movement of my fingers caused a sharp lance of pain. My skin was flaky.

Try again. "Mom—"

"Save it. Obviously I can't control you, and like I said I'm tired of trying. I'm worn-out. I'm so stressed I can't sleep anymore. I have headaches all the time now. I have no social life, no friends. I'm too busy chasing after you."

"I'm sorry," I whispered.

"I—I just can't do this anymore."

My head whipped up, and I peered at her with dread. "Don't send me back to rehab. Please. I didn't use. I didn't! All I want to do is make you proud."

"Stop," she bit out harshly, cutting me off again. "Just stop."

Tears filled my eyes, burning hotly. I scratched my arms, staring at her, trying to will her to believe me.

"The guy who brought you home told me he sent his own daughter to a special bootcamp for wayward teenagers." She faced me fully, her expression sad, determined. "He gave me the number. I've already called them. The director wasn't there, but he's going to call me as soon as he's in."

A gasp split my lips. "No. Don't do that. Don't send me away again. I just got back. Give me a chance. I'm trying to put my life together again."

She remained firm and unbending. "If they'll have you,

you're going. End of discussion." With that, she left my room, shutting the door with a soft click.

———

I spent the rest of the weekend in my room. I wanted to call and check on my friends, but I was forbidden from using the phone. No way would I disobey Mom now. I didn't need more trouble. Besides, they had to be okay. One or all of the news stations would have reported if anything had happened to them. Not that anyone had reported on the attack.

Which made me think of Ryan when he'd said, "So the media reports everything now?"

Perhaps they weren't as open and honest as I'd assumed.

What else didn't I know about?

I sighed. Most of my time was spent drinking water. Sucking it down, really, unable to get enough. I stared at the holophotos on my wall, animated pictures of me and Jamie playing in my backyard. We laughed and hugged each other.

They'd been snapped before either of us had started using.

She'd been the first to try it. When she told me how it numbed her inside and out, I'd begged for a taste. I'd been so happy at first. I'd thought nothing could hurt me. Now I knew.

I left my bedroom door open and caught my mother walking down the hall a few times. She'd look at me and tear up, but she wouldn't stop. Finally, on her fifth trip, I tried to make her talk to me. I hopped from my bed and rushed to the door, hands braced on the frame.

"We can work this out, Mom. We just have to try."

She halted abruptly, her back to me. She didn't turn around when she said, "We can't. We always end up here, with you strung out and me stressed out. I'm sorry."

I didn't know how to respond to that because it was true.

She laughed bitterly. "Maybe if I'd been a better wife, your dad wouldn't have taken off and started another family. He would be here, and you would obey him."

"We don't need him." I hadn't forgiven him for the way he'd left us without warning. I hadn't forgiven him for not contacting us since. It was as if we didn't exist to him anymore.

A part of me missed him, yes. Sometimes I cried for him, wondering what I'd done wrong, wondering if there was anything I could have done differently to make him stay. But I still hated him with everything inside of me. He'd tossed me aside like garbage.

Tears welled in my eyes, but I wiped them away with a clipped flick of my wrist. "We just need each other."

"Obviously, you need more." She walked away from me then.

Dejected, I tromped back to my bed and fell onto the mattress with a deep exhalation. The bed fit itself around my body, adjusting to my programmed comfort level. "Do a good deed," I muttered, "and be punished for the rest of your life. Yeah, that's fair."

Despite being cooped up and bored, the weekend passed quickly and Monday—doomsday—arrived all too soon.

The director of the "special bootcamp" finally called my mom. When the phone rang, I knew. Mom was in the kitchen cooking breakfast, so she used the phone in there. I was shaking as I silently tiptoed into the hallway to listen.

". . . drug addict," I heard her say. "She's willful and disobedient. She sneaks out, steals, and no telling what else." Bitter laugh.

A pause as she listened to the reply.

"I can't control her anymore, and I've lost the will to try."

Hearing her say that to someone else, something . . . broke me. Made me feel unwanted, unloved. Like a nuisance. She was abandoning me just as my dad had done. Only this time, with her, it was worse. It cut deeper.

Dad had packed his bags, stood in the doorway, and said good-bye without looking me in the eye. She, the woman who had hugged me, promised to always take care of me, and cried with me through the dark days that followed, knowing the pain I was in, was now doing the same.

"Cs, Ds, and Fs," my mom said. She must have been asked for my grades. "I know they're bad, but she's a smart girl when she's not using and her grades were getting better."

So why are you sending me away? Give me another chance.

"Yes," my mom said. "She's resourceful."

Pause.

"Yes. She can be forceful."

My brow wrinkled in confusion. What did that have to do with anything?

"Why are you asking me these questions?" Mom demanded, parroting my thoughts. "What does any of this matter? She needs help with drug use, not a personality adjustment."

A few minutes passed, my mom muttering "uh-huh" every other heartbeat of time. Finally she hung up and I slinked back to my room, waiting until the tears dried from my eyes and I wasn't shaking quite so badly before heading into the kitchen.

I didn't want her to know I'd overheard, so I didn't mention the phone call.

She didn't, either.

When she served breakfast, I accepted with a polite "thank you." I didn't know what else to say to her. What *could* I say?

"Eat and go to school," was her only response. She marched to the sink to wash the dishes in dry enzyme spray, keeping her back to me.

I blinked in surprise. Had she changed her mind about taking me to camp then? Or had they turned her down and didn't want to deal with me, either?

I didn't know how to make her understand that I'd changed. I wasn't the addict I used to be. I'm trying, I wanted to scream. More than that, I still wanted to find Ryan—and

Allison, too—drag them in front of her and force them to explain what had really happened that night.

Not that *I* fully understood what had happened.

"I don't want you to be late," Mom prompted.

"Are you going to drive me?"

"Not this time."

"All right then." Silence. "I guess this is good-bye."

"Yep."

"I love you," I called as I headed out the door and to the bus stop.

She didn't say a word.

I paused outside, waiting for her to say *something* at least. She never did. I tried not to let that bother me on the way to school. Cars whizzed past me. I saw old crumbling homes, then new homes with high-tech, robotic security systems. My mom always looked at those houses longingly when we drove past. We'd lived in a similar neighborhood when my dad had been with us.

New Chicago High finally came into view. One of the newer buildings, it was silver, towering, and wide. Each window and door was equipped with automatic shade to prevent people from seeing inside, a metal detector, and a computer that logged the identity of everyone who entered or left.

Every school was the exact same. No colors except silver, no team name (they'd been deemed "derogatory"). There were sports teams, of course, but they were strictly for humans since certain aliens and their abilities were considered "unfair."

There was a smattering of Arcadians that attended my school, the race known for their white hair, violet eyes, and psychic abilities. There were a few Terans, who were catlike (with fur, pointed ears, and scratchy tongues), and one Mec, a lanky thing that was all white, even its eyes.

I'd never really spent time with any of them. And now, more than ever, I didn't want to.

I entered Comp II, my first class of the day, experiencing a jolt of surprise when I spotted Jamie in back. She looked healthy, unscathed. Maneuvering around a too-slow student— who jumped out of the way so she wouldn't have to touch me, making me feel even lower—I quickened my step and slid into the chair directly across from Jamie's.

My backpack slapped against my side as I dropped it onto the floor.

"Hey," Jamie said, smiling when she spied me. She looked beautiful, well rested, and was wearing a black corset top and black cobweb pants.

"Are you okay?" I didn't waste time with idle conversation.

She frowned in confusion. "Yeah. Why wouldn't I be?"

Why wouldn't she be? *Uh, because we were attacked by aliens. Because you drank enough Breathless to kill ten humans.* "Do you remember anything about Friday night?"

"Yeah," she repeated. She laughed. "It was utterly—" Pause. She bit her bottom lip as she searched for the right word. "Amazing!"

O-kay. Not the word I would have chosen. "What about

the Sybilins? They would have killed you if Ryan and Allison hadn't fought them off."

For several seconds, Jamie didn't speak, just regarded me as if I needed to return to Chateau Insano for another round of therapy. Then her red glossed lips lifted in a slow smile. "I thought you were turning on us, but you flew that night, too, and hallucinated. God, it's so good to have you back."

"Wait." I held up my hand in a bid for silence. I could accept that she didn't recall the Sybilins or the ensuing battle. I knew what I had seen, I knew I hadn't done drugs, and it hadn't been a hallucination on my part. What I couldn't accept was everyone assuming I was using again. "I didn't use."

Her smile widened. "Sure you didn't."

I ground my teeth together. "How did you get home?"

Jamie's shoulder lifted in a delicate shrug, and she hooked several dark curls behind her ear. "Some asshole cop brought me home. He lectured me for flying the entire drive. Blah, blah, blah. I blacked out after a while and woke up yesterday morning in bed."

That sounded familiar.

"My parents almost had a breakdown when I woke up, since the officer had told them I'd 'abused Onadyn.'" She fluttered her lashes innocently. "Of course, someone must have spiked my drink because I would never do such a thing."

I opened my mouth to reply, but Mrs. Howard strode into the room, the door automatically closing behind her with a snap. "Good morning, class." She was all business. A black tailored pant suit, hair slicked back from her face, no-nonsense tone. "Take out your computers and click to page one hundred and sixteen of your Comp II book."

Several students groaned.

Jamie's computer already rested on top of her desk, so she punched a series of buttons. A blue square crystallized directly above the keyboard, dappled like water but thicker. Almost like jelly. Her fingers then keyed in the appropriate code and page number and the words materialized, small and black, perfectly legible.

I searched my backpack, but didn't see my computer. Dread filling me, I straightened. I must have left it at home.

"Phoenix Germaine, take out your book," Mrs. Howard commanded. "We have a lot to cover today and not a lot of time to do it."

I met her very stern stare, not allowing myself to flinch. "I don't have it. I'm sorry."

Her lips thinned with displeasure. "That is unacceptable, Miss Germaine. Without your computer, you cannot take notes. Without taking notes, you will fail the next test and you, my dear, cannot afford to fail."

Chairs skidded backward as everyone turned to look at me. Some were snickering, some were smirking. My cheeks flushed. Thankfully, a knock sounded at the door, saving me from having to utter a reply.

Mrs. Howard pressed a button on a remote, and the darkened screen in the center of the door cleared, revealing the face of Principal Edgars and—I couldn't make out who was with him, only the slash of black. Mrs. Howard pressed another button and the door slid open.

Edgars strode inside, flanked by a tall, well-muscled man I didn't recognize, as well as an equally tall redheaded female. They stopped in the center and pivoted toward the class. Oh, no. No, no, no. There was only one reason people like that would be in this school.

My heart drummed in my chest so hard I feared my ribs would crack. *Please don't say my na—*

"Phoenix Germaine," the principal said in his deep, raspy voice. He had plain mocha features, mocha-colored eyes, and they swept over the students until landing on me. "Gather your supplies and step into the hall."

Once again everyone faced me. My mouth went dry, as if the Sybilins were here sucking out every ounce of moisture. I hadn't gotten out of camp, after all.

The two strangers didn't say a word, just eyed me up and down, inspecting me as if I were a house or car they were thinking about buying. I gulped. I couldn't believe my mom had really done it; I couldn't believe she was sending me away without saying good-bye.

Tears stung my eyes, but I brushed them away. *Don't cry, don't cry, don't cry.* I'd be strong. I'd be okay.

"What's going on?" Jamie whispered behind her hand.

How long until I saw her again? How long would I be forced to stay at camp for a crime I hadn't committed?

"Phoenix?" Jamie said, uncertain.

"My life is crumbling, that's what's happening." I stood on shaky legs and hefted my backpack onto my shoulder.

"You won't need that," the male stranger said, speaking for the first time since entering the room.

Why not? I wanted to ask, but didn't. I was afraid of the answer. Biting my lower lip, I dropped the pack to the ground.

"Mrs. Howard will take care of your belongings," Edgars said.

I faced straight ahead, then allowed my feet to follow the path of my gaze. I didn't look left or right, didn't acknowledge the people staring at me, wondering. All too soon, I was standing in front of Edgars and the strangers. I'd fought the Sybilins and won; I wouldn't let this defeat me.

"She's being arrested again?" a student muttered behind me.

"Let's hope so," someone answered.

Edgars nodded at me. There was pity in his dark eyes. "Good luck, kid." He pivoted on his heel and stalked out of the room.

The strangers, however, waited for me. The man even motioned to the door with his chin.

I squared my shoulders. "If you wanted to see my ass, mister, you should have just said so." I think his lips twitched, nearly spreading into a smile, but I didn't hang around to study him more closely. I sashayed into the hall as if I hadn't a care in the world.

I'd never been so miserable, but I wouldn't let them know how close I was to breaking down.

"To the front entrance," he commanded, still behind me but closer than I'd realized. His voice was somehow familiar to me.

I didn't look back as I continued to walk, never slowing my pace. "Where's this *special* camp located, anyway?" That's what my mom had called it, a special camp for wayward teens. Ugh.

"Nowhere," the man answered cryptically.

I snorted. "Hell?"

"Some would say so, yes."

Oh, goody.

The hallways were deserted. That wasn't surprising. During class, rooms were put on lockdown. No one was allowed inside or out without a fingerprint scan and permission from the principal. "I don't belong at your camp, you know," I said when we reached the glass doors that lead outside. They were shaded, so I couldn't see the parking lot.

"Maybe, maybe not. We'll soon find out." In the next instant, he grabbed my upper arm and spun me around.

I didn't have time to protest. Didn't have time to curse or fight.

A cloth was shoved over my head, and the world around me went black. I was so startled, a moment passed before I realized what had happened. Then my heart kicked into gear, realization hit, and fury and fear pounded through me. "What are you doing? Let me go!"

"Don't worry," the man said. "This is for your own protection."

I struggled against his hold. "Let. Me. Go!"

"Calm down. It'll all be over soon, Phoenix."

I stilled, gulped. Panicked. What would be over soon? My life? Dear God. What had my mom gotten me into?

4

It'll all be over soon . . . I tried to rip the hood from my head, but my hands were slapped away. I erupted once again, kicking and hitting with every ounce of my strength, striking blindly, sometimes connecting with my target.

He grunted.

No way was I going to be treated this way. No way was I going to be led—where? In front of a firing squad? Into a room filled with people who wanted me to be their piñata? All to punish me for a crime I hadn't committed.

"I did nothing wrong!" I growled. "For the first time I did everything right, damn it. I don't deserve this."

"Be still, Phoenix, and be quiet." The man was panting as he tried to subdue me, but his voice was surprisingly gentle.

"I've told you twice already. Let me go!"

"I'll gag you if I have to," he said. In the next instant, my arms were banded behind my back, preventing me from reaching up. Laserbands bonded to skin, and would cut to the bone if I attempted to pull them off.

My teeth ground together as I continued to kick. I even tried to ram him with the back of my head, but I never made contact. The man—I needed a name for him—must have dodged my flailing limbs.

Finally he picked me up and threw me over his shoulder. The scent of pine and . . . *roses* filled my nose. An odd smell for a man, especially a tough, hard one like this. Roses. I'd call him Roses.

"The others didn't act this way," Roses said.

"She's going to be trouble," a sweet female voice said.

"The good ones always are," he responded.

"I told you, I didn't do anything wrong. I don't deserve this."

Roses chuckled, deep and rich. "You're right. You don't deserve it, but if you try hard enough and apply yourself, you just might."

Confused by his words, I paused. Then, suddenly, warm air was kissing my arms, my exposed midriff. We were outside, I realized. I could hear cars zooming past on a nearby road. I wanted to see, but couldn't make out anything through the black hood.

"Where are you taking me?" Straight to camp? Probably. They weren't going to let me pack my things, my holophotos. I'd be cut off from everything and everyone I knew and loved.

"We're taking you to a whole new world, sugar. Just sit back and enjoy the ride," Sweet Voice said.

"Enjoy? Enjoy! You can stuff your 'enjoy' right up your as—" My words jammed to a halt as I was chucked onto a hard, uncushioned seat. A door slammed, and then there was only silence. I wiggled and squirmed, trying to dislodge the hood without moving my arms and disturbing the laserbands.

"That won't do you any good," someone said. A new voice. A girlish, almost purring voice. "The hood is bonded to your clothing just like the laserbands are bonded to your skin."

I froze, tried to force my gaze past the black fibers of the hood to see *something*. Anything. Again, only darkness greeted me. "Who are you?"

"A recruit, like you," she replied, and there was a blend of happiness and frustration in her tone. "My name's Kitten."

Was Kitten hooded, too? I asked and she replied with an angry yes. The knowledge calmed me for some reason— perhaps because I was not alone in this. Still, I wished I could see who I was talking to. "Why'd they blindfold us like this?"

A pause. A rustle of clothing, as if she was shrugging. "If we aren't accepted, we'll be sent home. This way, we won't know the location of the camp."

"Accepted?"

"Yeah. Into the program."

"I'm still lost," I said. "Why do we have to be accepted?"

"Only the strong survive and all that crap."

Great. Visions of being locked in a room with other "delinquent" kids and forced to fight to the death filled my head. Although, I might willingly take a beating if it meant being considered weak and sent home.

"What's your name, new girl?" the purring voice demanded.

"Phoenix."

"Wait," an unfamiliar male voice said. "You were named after a mythical bird?"

My head whipped to the left, in the direction of the new speaker. A boy. "Who are you? And how many more kids are in here?"

"I'm Bradley, and we're it. It's just the three of us. A ménage," he replied happily.

The car suddenly jostled into motion, flinging me forward and causing my bands to pull tight. Grimacing, I righted myself.

"No one wants to hear you speak, Bradie boy," Kitten said in that scratchy voice of hers.

"Like that's ever stopped me. I can't believe we've got a bird and a cat in the car." Bradley chuckled. "I guess that makes me animal control. Nice."

"I'm a Teran," Kitten said tightly, "not a cat. And if I hear you call me a cat one more time, I'll scratch your eyes out. Understand?"

"Oh, I understand. I just don't think you'll like *what* I'm understanding, which is that you can't wait to get your hands on me."

She hissed.

He laughed, but there was a trace of trepidation in the sound. "So . . . what do you know about Terans, Bird?"

"Don't call me that," I snapped.

"Gotta distract myself somehow," he muttered.

He was right. We had to distract ourselves however possible. Otherwise I might scream. "I know some Terans are covered in fur," I said, answering his question. "Others simply have pointed pupils and pointed ears."

"Ever seen one in real life?" he asked.

"Yes."

"Ever seen one attack a human?"

"No."

"That's enough," Kitten said, butting in. "You sound like an alienphobe."

Did *I* fear aliens? "I'm not," I said with assurance. I didn't have a problem with the otherworlders who lived among us. For the most part. The Sybilins, well, I wanted *them* dead.

"If a girl is hot," Bradley said, and I was sure he was leering, "I don't care what race she is."

"I'd already guessed that about you," I replied dryly.

"Already wanting a piece of me, too, I bet."

Kitten and Bradley continued to spar, ignoring me. I leaned against the back of my seat and drew in a breath. The air inside my hood was surprisingly fresh, light, as if there were air pockets sewn into the material. "What do you guys know about this bootcamp?" I asked, cutting into their heated conversation.

"Now why'd you have to go and bring that up?" Bradley asked with a moan. "I was doing a good job forgetting where I was and where I was headed."

"I don't know a lot," Kitten admitted. "What I know, I know because my sister graduated from it several years ago. See, every three months a panel of—judges, I guess you could call them—picks a few students to come and basically try out. Half are sent home in the first few weeks."

One, try out for a drug rehab? That was craziness. Two, half were sent home? Maybe I'd be one of the lucky half.

"So what'd you do to get sent there?" Kitten asked.

Another rustle of clothing. "I didn't do nothin'," Bradley said. "One day I was playing virtual football with a group of Arcadians, the next I was blindfolded and shoved into a car with two sexy-sounding hotties."

I rolled my eyes. The fact that he hadn't been caught doing drugs surprised me. Wasn't this camp for drug addicts?

"I'm here because I beat the shit out of an Ell Rollis," Kitten said. "And I'm about to beat the shit out of a human boy."

"Bring it on," Bradley said.

Ell Rollis . . . I flipped through my mental files, but couldn't picture one. Sensing my confusion, Kitten said, "They're huge. Like two musclemen fused together—even the women are like that. And they don't have a nose. I think they breathe from their ears or something." She purred low in her throat, as if her words delighted her. "Beating an Ell Rollis makes you an asskicker extraordinarie."

To win against a creature like that, Kitten had to be gargantuan, but the Terans I'd seen had been lithe and small and graceful. So . . . the camp was for fighters and—in Bradley's case—perverts, as well as flyers. Not wanting to admit where I fell in that equation, I kept my mouth shut about *my* crimes.

Bradley chuckled, saying, "That's a fight I would have liked to have seen. I bet there was no pulling hair or biting." He paused. "Wait, scratch that. Biting would have been good."

I'd only known the boy a few minutes, but I kind of expected the comment from him. "I wonder what they'll do to us," I said. "The camp people, I mean. Not the Ell Rollises."

"Who knows?" Kitten shifted in her seat. "A few tolerance classes, anger management, probably. That kind of crap. My sister never told me about that part. Said she was sworn to secrecy."

I'd endured enough of those types of classes in rehab. *Tell us your feelings, Phoenix. Visualize a meadow of happiness, Phoenix. Deep breath in and deep breath out, letting all of your negative energy out, Phoenix.* What a waste of time. What a nightmare.

Nothing was more boring.

The car suddenly twisted, pushing me to the left. I couldn't catch myself since my hands were locked behind my back and ended up sliding into a warm body.

"Oh yeah," Bradley said. "Me likie likie. Feel free to stay like this."

When he didn't try to palm my breasts, I knew beyond a doubt that he was banded like me and the pair hadn't been lying. I straightened with a muttered, "Perv."

"No better way to be."

"One day a girl is going to cut out your tongue," Kitten told him.

"If she does it with her teeth, I'm surprisingly okay with that."

I held back a laugh.

After that, time passed in silence for a long while. Without the distraction, my mind wandered. What was my mom doing right now? Would I ever see my house again? Already a wave of homesickness hit me.

Finally Kitten sighed. "This sucks."

Yeah, it did. The waiting . . . the not knowing. . . . A few minutes later, the road became bumpy, jostling me up and down. "Where the hell are we?"

"The devil's playground, is my guess," Kitten said. "Although the entire last year of my life has been spent in that area, so this must just be another section."

"I'd say we're in heaven." Bradley belted out a laugh, but it once again held a trace of trepidation. "I'm betting this camp is co-ed and life just doesn't get any better than that."

"God save me from perverts," I said, trying to keep the amusement from my voice.

Bradley just laughed again.

"You don't need God this time," Kitten replied. "It'll be my pleasure to save you from Bradie boy."

Bradley cleared his throat. "I'm really looking forward to your attempt, *Cat*."

Kitten hissed again. "I warned you. You won't know when and you won't know where, but you'll pay for that."

"Cat-y, cat, cat."

I pressed my lips together to smother a chuckle. Thank the Lord I hadn't been shoved into this car alone. The battling pair had saved me from untold worry.

Unfortunately, a sharp turn, several more bumps, and a jarring stop later, we arrived at our destination. My stomach clenched, and I lost all hint of amusement, no longer able to keep the worry at bay.

"We're here," Kitten said, sounding nervous.

"Yeah," Bradley said, his voice broken.

We once again lapsed into silence, this one laden with heavy tension. My nerves sparked, a little raw. What was going to happen next?

The slide of a door sounded, then footsteps. Then . . . nothing. Wait. A rustle of wind, the sway of trees. The chirp of insects. My hands began to sweat. I wanted the hood and laserbands removed *now*! These feelings of helplessness and vulnerability were almost as terrible as being taken from home, from the only life I knew.

"All right, you three," Roses said. I think he brushed his hands together in relish. "It's showtime."

"What, you're going to make us sing and dance?" Kitten demanded.

"If you make the girls dance," Bradley said, "can I take off my hood and watch?"

"We're not performing monkeys," I muttered.

Roses laughed with genuine amusement. "You will be if I tell you to be."

"We'll see about that," I told him. "Maybe *you'll* be the one to dance."

"Trouble," Sweet Voice said. "Told you she'd be trouble. She's already back talking."

Roses said, "This is what's going to happen, children. You'll be taken inside one at a time and led into a room where you will be interviewed. You will answer each question honestly."

My brows arched. Not that anyone could see my expression. "And if we don't?"

Pause.

Then, "Answer and answer honestly," he said with an ominous edge, "because you won't like what happens if you remain silent or lie. And before you ask how we'll know if you're lying, I'll tell you the answer. We know everything."

My stomach twisted into a thousand tiny, painful knots.

"Why ask us anything, then?" I so did not want to be here, playing cloak and dagger games while answering questions about my life. And they would be about my life, my choices. I knew it. They always were.

"Since you're so eager to speak," Roses said, "you can go first, Phoenix. The rest of you will wait here. Don't try to leave the vehicle. I've already posted guards at the doors."

Someone reached inside and latched onto my upper arm. I was dragged out of the car and onto my feet. My boots sank into something soft. Grass, probably. The darkness of the hood disoriented me, and I wobbled. "Remove the blindfold, at least."

"You'll wear it until you're deemed worthy to take it off," Roses said. "Otherwise, I'd have to blind you some other way." His harsh tone suggested he'd just go ahead and rip out my eyes.

"The hood is fine." Logically, I knew he wouldn't hurt me. Or rather, *hoped* he wouldn't hurt me. Camp counselors weren't allowed to injure their charges, were they?

That didn't drain my fear, however. I couldn't see his expression, didn't know him and what he was capable of doing—didn't know if the law even mattered to him.

I wasn't even one hundred percent certain what type of camp this was, despite—or maybe because of—Kitten's explanation. This was like no camp I'd ever encountered before. Everything from the hoods to the laserbands to the absolute secrecy was beyond my realm of experience.

Roses ushered me inside a building. I knew the moment I went indoors because the air changed. Suddenly there was no breeze. Only sterile-smelling air, as if some kind of cleaner had been used, blocking any hint of fragrance.

We turned once, twice, stalking down a long hallway, was my guess. I didn't hear other footsteps, didn't hear other voices.

"Nervous?" Roses asked me.

"No," I answered with false bravado.

He *tsk*ed under his tongue. "Lying already. I warned you about that."

"What are you going to do? Kick me out?" *Pretty please with a cherry on top.*

"Is that what you want? To be kicked out?" He *tsk*ed again. "I expected better from you, Phoenix."

He was the first to expect anything good from me then. "I expected to finish the day at school, go home, do my homework, and take a nap in my own bed."

"That's sad. You should expect more for yourself."

"And disappoint myself as well as my mom? No thanks."

He didn't say anything else. A few seconds later, he stopped. He released my upper arm, only to grip both of my shoulders and guide me a few inches to the side. "Sit," he said.

Something hard bumped into the backs of my knees. A chair, I hoped. I eased down, concerned that he'd jerk the seat away at any moment and laugh. He didn't and I was able to settle comfortably on top of it.

My ears twitched when I heard someone sigh. The sigher was a few feet away, I estimated. There was a shuffle of papers and the squeak of syn-leather.

"Welcome, Miss Germaine," a deep, scary voice said. "So glad you could make it. Now, why don't we get started, hmm?"

"Get started with what?" I asked, even though Roses had already told me I'd be interviewed. I was nervous and stalling for time.

He answered me anyway. "Why, deciding whether you live or die."

5

"State your name," the man said only two seconds after he threatened my life.

I didn't reply. Couldn't. There was a lump the size of New Chicago in my throat. This wasn't right. These people should not be allowed to threaten me like that.

I didn't want to be here. I wanted to go home. *To what? A mom who's washed her hands of me? Yeah, good luck with that.* Anything was better than this, though.

"State your name," he insisted.

Again, I remained silent. I found myself really missing my dad all of a sudden. Why couldn't I be one of those girls with a father who rushed to her defense? A father who broke down doors and broke the law to save his little angel? Instead I had no one who would rescue me.

I was on my own.

"State. Your. Name."

There was such unbending command in his voice that my lips parted and words spilled out before I could stop myself—though I still didn't obey. "You already know it. This is stupid."

"This is your last chance. State your name." "Or suffer the consequences" drifted through the air unsaid.

"Phoenix Ann Germaine." *Just get this over with,* I thought. *Answer their questions and get out of this hood. Get* home. I didn't like that people were watching me, judging me, especially since I didn't know how many were here or even what they looked like—or what they were doing.

Each one of them could have a gun aimed at me, finger poised on the trigger. With that thought, sweat beaded over my skin. A cold sweat that somehow heated my blood. The breath in my lungs fragmented, making it hard to concentrate.

"You're seventeen years old?" a clipped female voice asked.

"Yes." Almost eighteen, I nearly added, but didn't want to prolong the conversation in any way. I now knew there were at least three people in the room with me. Deep Voice, Roses, and the woman. I'd give them no more than they asked for. No elaboration.

"You are an Onadyn addict," another voice said, this one male. "Yes?"

That made four people. The entire room tapered to quiet. Not even the rustle of clothes or paper could be heard. I could feel their eyes burning into me, waiting for my answer.

My jaw clenched. "Former addict," I gritted out.

A chair squeaked. Murmurs. "Why is she even here?" that same male said—the one who'd asked me if I was an addict. "This is ridiculous. A user is always a user."

A minute passed; I strained to hear but he was never given an answer.

"Do you still use, Phoenix?" a hard feminine voice asked.

If I answered yes, would I be sent home or be forced to remain? Several heart-stopping minutes passed while I considered my response. In the end, I opted for the truth. "No. I told you. I'm a *former* user."

Pause.

Then, "When was your last dose?"

"A few months ago," I answered, once again opting for honesty.

"Why should we believe you?"

Surprise swept through me, potent and strong. Ryan was here. I'd recognize that raspy tone anywhere. He hadn't sounded insulting or sneering. No, he'd sounded expectant. Why?

And what was he doing here? Was he a counselor at the camp?

"Answer the question," Deep Voice commanded.

I shrugged. "My own mother doesn't trust me, so why should anyone else?" Not only had I used drugs, but I'd slept around, lied, and stolen. *No wonder Mom hadn't believed me,* I thought bitterly. I'd been a nightmare.

Maybe I did deserve this place.

I'm different now. Don't forget.

"I'd like to hear more about your mother. Do you hate her for not trusting you? Do you blame her?" another woman asked.

I shook my head. "No. I don't hate or blame her." She'd taken care of me for as long as she'd been able. I *was* hurt, I couldn't deny that. But they hadn't asked that, so I didn't say it.

"Are you angry with her?"

I paused, then answered honestly, "Yes."

"Why?"

"Because," I said.

"Because why?" Deep Voice insisted.

"Because she should have loved me enough to keep me. Because she should have loved me enough to try again. Because I'm an idiot. Is that what you want to hear?"

Someone chuckled. Ryan, I think, because the sound of it warmed me.

Still, I ran my tongue over my teeth. I didn't want to be amusing. I wanted to be dismissed. Except . . . more than leaving, I found that I wanted to know what Ryan was doing here. If he wasn't a counselor, had he been sent to the camp after that fight? If so, why was he allowed to be here during my interrogation?

"How do you feel about other-worlders, Phoenix?" Deep Voice asked.

I handled the switch in topics with ease. "Which ones?"

"All of them," was the flat response.

"Lumping every species into one category is like lumping all humans into one category. Some are different. Let's take this group, for instance. Each one of you is a bastard, but that doesn't mean the two kids in the car outside are bastards, as well."

A girl sucked in a breath. A guy cleared his throat.

"I want her out," someone muttered. "Finishing the interview is pointless."

"If we let her in and the others start to act like her . . ."

If my wrists had been free, I might have flipped the speaker off. Something about her irked me. She was so superior. "So, how many people are here?" I asked.

"A good agent can figure that out without the use of her eyes," a girl said. Allison Stone, I realized with another dose of shock.

She was here, too? Oh, that burned! And what did she mean, "agent"? "Why aren't I allowed to see any of you?"

"We'll ask the questions," Allison snapped.

"Well, then, I'll decide whether or not to answer," I replied in the same snotty tone she'd used.

"That's music to my ears, user."

"Allison," Deep Voice said. "Shut your mouth or leave. I allowed you to sit in because you're about to graduate and one day you'll help run this camp. Don't make me regret my decision."

She would help run it? "This is a joke, right? You're all actors trying to bring back that practical joke show."

No one replied.

"She has a serious attitude problem," I heard.

Again with the mutterings. I rolled my eyes. Not that they could see me.

"She'll be too hard to control," someone else offered.

"Yes, but she has passion." That came from Ryan. "She's had no training. She was drinking that night, but still fought the Sybilins like a highly trained agent. If she hadn't been there, we could have lost."

"Agent" . . . that was the second mention. What kind of agent?

"There's her drug problem to contend with."

"True."

"And it *will* be a problem. A big one."

They were speaking so quickly and so quietly, I had trouble making out who was saying what. But I offered, "No problem at all since it's a *former* drug problem. And if one of you told my mother that I was smoking Onadyn that night in the forest, I'll kill you."

"She's violent and bloodthirsty at least; I'll give her points for that," that clipped female voice said. And she sounded happy about the statement.

They *wanted* me to be violent and bloodthirsty? Really, what the hell kind of place was this?

"You always pick the violent ones, Mia," Deep Voice said. "I'm not sure this one's worth the effort, though."

Bastard. "Who are you people?" I demanded. I pulled on

the laser that bound my wrists together, trying to free myself so that I could remove the hood. But it hurt, and I stilled. Already the skin felt raw and irritated. Much more and I might lose a hand.

No thanks.

"We have a few more questions for you, little girl, then maybe you'll find out." Roses.

My mom often called me "little girl" and it irritated me every time. Ryan had called me that, too. I wanted to call this guy "old man," but didn't dare. For all I knew, he had a gun pointed at my temple like I'd first feared. Or maybe he had a knife balanced over my head, ready to drop at any moment.

"If she fails, kick her out," Mia said. "I want her to have a chance, at least."

"I've read her file, and she's got 'problem' written all over it." Sweet Voice. The woman who had helped bring me here. Only she didn't sound sweet anymore. She sounded pissed. "I don't want to mess with her. New recruits are always a challenge, but she's hopeless."

That hurt. I didn't know the woman, but her words hurt. I drew in a breath, wishing once again that I could see through the fibers of the hood. As it was, I couldn't even see a single ray of light.

"Could you kill?"

Silence.

"Phoenix, could you kill someone?" the one called Mia asked.

"What, you're talking to the lowly little girl now?"

"Yes," she said without remorse.

"I don't know," I replied honestly. The logical side of my brain told me that no one in their right mind would want a girl to admit to violent tendencies. In the real world, that would get me placed in isolation or lockup. After the "violent and bloodthirsty" comment, though . . .

That night in the forest, I could have killed. Had wanted to kill. The Sybilins were evil, vile, destructive. They shouldn't be allowed to live or they'd hurt more people. But, would I be able to kill someone—something—else? A living being? "With or without provocation?" I asked.

"Either."

I sighed. "Maybe. Probably."

A pause.

"Are you afraid of pain?"

"What do you think?" I answered dryly.

The rustle of paper, the shift of a body. "Let's see." Deep Voice paused. "In the tenth grade, you were in a fight with a human female double your weight. You required sixteen stitches in your neck."

"So."

"So, most people are so afraid of pain they would not have challenged—or accepted the challenge—of someone larger than themselves."

"She knifed me," I said, recalling that day. I'd been walk-ing to class, minding my own business, and a girl I'd never spoken with had reached out and sliced my neck with a plastic kitchen knife she'd sharpened and honed.

"He's mine," she'd screamed.

Apparently, she'd wanted the boy I'd gotten high with the night before. Rumors had surfaced that we'd had sex, and she'd gone a little crazy. The moment I'd realized what she'd done, I had jumped her. Attacked, full force, unconcerned about her size or my lack of size. I'd had only one thought: stop her. She'd been aiming for my face, I'd later learned, wanting to scar me.

I had a scar, but it stretched the left side of my neck and was covered when I wore my hair down.

"In eleventh grade, you broke three bones in your wrist," Deep Voice continued.

"Yeah. So?"

"Again with the so," Roses muttered. "Explain how that came about."

My fingers were beginning to swell from lack of movement so I flexed them as I spoke. "I was in a fight. Again."

"For?"

"A new girl at school called my friend a bitch. I reacted. It was dumb," I added. But I hadn't thought so at the time. I'd been coming down from a high, and I'd been enraged by everything and everyone. I would have attacked anyone for any ridiculous reason.

"Any other questions for this girl?" Deep Voice asked.

I knew he wasn't talking to me.

Shuffle of feet, the squeak of wheels. I could picture these people—however many there were—huddling together and . . . yes, they were whispering. I heard the frantic rasp of their voices. I knew they were discussing me, my answers.

"I don't think any more are necessary," Roses said with finality.

Even though I strained, I couldn't make out anyone's response. Several minutes passed, and the whispering session became more heated. What were they saying? Kick me out and send me home? *Please, please, please.*

"I have a question," Allison said loudly. Her words echoed off the walls, in my ears.

"Let's hear it," Deep Voice told her.

"It's not a question, really, but a situation. I'd like to know what she'd do."

"Let's hear it," I said, mimicking the authority Deep Voice used.

Ryan chuckled again, and again I felt the warmth of it.

"You're in a dark alley," Allison said stiffly. "You're alone. You have no weapons. A group of Outers stumble upon you, and they obviously want your blood spilled over the dirty concrete. What do you do?"

Everyone went quiet. The air became heavy with tension.

"Why don't I have weapons?" I asked just to be difficult. She was trying to trip me up, I knew it. There had to be a right answer and a wrong answer, and everyone was waiting to hear which one I'd give. While a small part of me wanted to give the wrong answer so I'd (hopefully) be sent home, a big part of me wanted to give the right answer and knock her off her I'm-so-superior throne.

"You just don't!"

"Not even a barrette from my hair?"

"No," she barked.

More chuckles. Not just from Ryan.

"What about a rock from the ground?" I asked.

"No! Nothing. Just you and the men."

"Are they armed?"

"Yes!"

"Are they tall or short?"

"Tall! Stop stalling. What would you do?"

"Look, I'm not stalling." And I wasn't—anymore. I think I knew the right answer. There was no way in hell I'd be caught in a dark alley with no weapons. But I didn't say that. "I'm just trying to get a clear picture of the situation. As to what I'd do, well, I know what I *wouldn't* do. I wouldn't fight them since they're tall men who could probably beat my bones into powder."

When I didn't continue, Deep Voice prompted me. "So what *would* you do?"

I shrugged. "I'd memorize their physical descriptions if possible, maybe grab something from them, a piece of clothing, a wallet, so they could be tracked later, and then I'd run like hell." Cowardly? Maybe. But staying alive was a little more important than looking brave.

Allison snorted. I guess that's the answer she'd wanted to hear. "Would you smoke a Snow Angel while you were at it?"

Before I could reply, Mia said, "I want her. She's just what this place needs. Logical, passionate, and determined. And like I said, you can kick her out if she doesn't work."

Deep Voice sighed. "I knew you'd say that. But I have to agree with the others. The drug use . . . if she were to cause any of the others to become addicted . . ."

Sweet Voice piped in. "This is a stressful program and an addict almost always caves during stress."

"How many times do I have to say it? We'll test her. Every day if necessary. Until she fails, let's give her a chance. People with passion don't come around often, and how many of you can claim to have led perfect lives?"

"Mia—"

"Boss, she's got what it takes. I know it, and you know it. A chance is all I want for her."

Silence. I imagined them staring each other down—because I didn't want to think about how their words were making me feel. Half-elated, half-beaten down.

"Well, it's settled then," Deep Voice finally said with a sigh. "She stays."

In the next instant, my blindfold was removed. Light pierced my eyes, and I had to blink against the blinding brightness. Several strands of pale hair fell over my face. I blew them back.

With a quick jerk, my hands were free, and I was able to

reach up and scrub. The action hurt. My shoulders screamed in protest, and my hands trembled wildly.

I didn't show a single ounce of my pain, though. I wouldn't let these people see any hint of weakness after they'd stripped my past bare and made it fodder for everyone in the room. Only one person here seemed to want me. The only other time I'd felt this low was when I sobered and recalled the way I'd treated my mom that day at school.

What I hated most, however, was that they were right. I *could* start using again at any moment. I always had in the past. I liked to think I'd resist no matter what, but . . .

Finally my vision cleared. I was unable to control my reaction as everyone came into focus. I gasped, shock pounding through me.

I was in the center of an all-white cell. There were no exits. Lights hung from the ceiling, glowing, illuminating. A table circled me, pinning me in except for a small gap by the door. At each section of the table was a human. And there were fifteen of them.

Roses stood beside me. Ryan, who looked as sexy as I remembered, was watching me with grim determination and . . . admiration? His dark hair was rumpled, and his bright blue eyes were fringed by feathered black lashes.

My stomach tightened at the sight of him.

Allison, who looked prettier than ever, was seated next to him. She was frowning at me. Beside her was an older man with thick silver hair and lightly tanned (and slightly wrinkled) skin. He wore a pair of black glasses over his eyes.

On his other side was Sweet Voice. She, too, looked upset.

There were several people I didn't recognize. A woman with long black hair and blue eyes that were so clear they were almost purple. She was beautiful, like a ballerina. Delicate. A woman with brown hair, hazel eyes, and physically perfect features was next to her.

I'd never seen such loveliness in real life.

The rest of the audience was comprised of men. All tall, all muscled, all fierce. All savagely handsome. It was as if everyone in the cell had come to life from a holophoto. And each and every one of them was now studying me as if they wanted to eat me for lunch and spit out my bones.

One by one, they said, "Welcome." Only a few sounded happy.

Sunglasses splayed his arms and smiled. "They've all welcomed you to A.I.R. training camp, but allow me to do so, as well. Welcome to your new home, Phoenix. For the moment, anyway."

6

I wasn't given time to react or learn the names of my interrogators. Immediately after issuing that eerie "welcome"—that wasn't really a welcome with the "for the moment, anyway" attached—Sunglasses motioned for Roses to usher me into another all-white cell, this one empty, devoid of even the circular table.

Roses did as he'd been commanded, the wall splitting open and leading into a hallway that lead into another cell. He deposited me there, leaving me alone and locking me inside without a word.

I stood there, shock pounding through me. How had this happened?

I'd just been recruited for A.I.R. Alien Investigation and Removal. Me. Phoenix Germaine. A troublemaker, a former drug addict, and a girl who was unwanted by her own parents. An agent.

Me, I thought again. It was . . . it was . . . I didn't know what it was.

A.I.R. agents were the elite, the very best. They were tough and respected, immortalized in movies. And they wanted me to fight otherworldly crime, racing through the night and dodging laser beams and pyre-fire?

A little dizzy, I leaned against the padded wall—padded for the crazies?—and slid to the floor. I anchored my head in my upraised hands. Deep breath in. Deep breath out. My mind frazzled with lightning speed, a whorl of thoughts and confusion.

Did I really want this for myself?

I was only seventeen. I hadn't yet graduated high school. How could *I* be an agent? It had to be one of the most dangerous occupations there was. Look at the Sybilins we had fought.

What if I encountered worse?

Was that what I wanted to deal with every day? Talk about stress.

I'd never really considered my future. With my grades, college hadn't seemed possible. With my record, most jobs were out.

"Dear God." The questions during the interview began, at last, to make sense. Could I kill? Could I deal with pain?

A.I.R. agents fought without backing down, no matter the choice of weapons, no matter the injury inflicted upon them. That was why they were considered the best.

Even the most depraved of predators trembled at the sight of them.

What would my mother say if she knew where I was and what I'd been recruited to do? *Did* she know? She hadn't breathed one word about A.I.R. Did she assume this was simply a boot camp as she'd lead me to believe?

Half of me thought, if she knew, she'd finally be proud of her little girl, trying to make a difference in the world. The other half of me, well, imagined her disappointment at learning her daughter was supposed to kill things for a living.

Which was the right supposition? I just didn't know.

Lost in thought as I was, I didn't realize the wall had split and someone stood there, watching me. "It's a lot to take in, I know," a voice suddenly said.

I gasped and whipped my attention to the side. Ryan leaned against the side of the doorway. He was frowning, his arms crossed over his chest.

"Yes," I managed, hating how breathless I sounded.

He stepped toward me, and the door closed behind him. My heart kicked into gear as I hopped to my feet. "What are you doing here?"

"I came to see how you're doing."

"Not so good." More than the tone of my voice, I hated how hot he looked, how rugged, because he was older than me and probably viewed me as nothing more than a little girl. A druggie, loser little girl at that.

"So . . ." He closed the rest of the distance between us and stuffed his hands in his pockets. Our gazes met and held, his blue against my brown—a blank slate against . . . what emotion was I showing him? Confusion? Shock? Pleasure that he'd come to see me? "What do you think?" he asked.

My brow furrowed. "Help me out here. Exactly what are you asking my opinion about? What I think about you? Or the camp? Or A.I.R.? Or even the entire messed-up situation of being taken from my school and brought here in secret? What about the fact that you let my mom think I got high that night?" I added, anger heating my blood.

"I'm sorry about that. I didn't want it to happen, but I didn't know your past at the time. I didn't know she'd just assume . . ."

My cheeks burned.

"We couldn't tell her the truth, Phoenix. The rest of the world can't know what goes on with predatory aliens. They'll panic. They'll loot. They'll kill innocent Outers on sight. You can't even tell your mother what we do here. Very few even know it exists. She thinks she sent you to an undisclosed location for tough love drug treatment."

"Yeah, well, where do the parents of the other kids think their children have been sent?"

"Programs for the gifted, the talented. Whatever fits their situation."

How embarrassing for me. They were gifted and talented; I was the only loser. "Anyone like me ever been admitted before?"

"No. You're the first. When Mia heard about you, she demanded you be brought in." Ryan cleared his throat. "We don't have much time. Let's talk about A.I.R."

A minute passed in silence, and I used very second to think of a witty response. Nothing came to me. "I have so many questions. If I decide to stay here, where will I live? What's going to be required of me? What aliens will I be required to fight, and will I have to kill them *now*?"

"You'll live here, with the other trainees. You'll be required to work hard, demonstrate loyalty and dedication. No drugs. You'll fight . . . no one," he said. He shrugged. "Not yet, at least."

My jaw clenched at the "no drugs" bit. I didn't comment, though. I reached up and massaged the back of my neck. "I don't understand. No fighting? But—"

"You have to learn how to fight before you're sent into the field." He leaned his shoulder against the wall, and I caught the scent of woods and soap. A wonderful scent. The best I'd smelled so far. Better, even, than Roses.

"This place really is a training ground, then," I said. "Like that guy said."

Ryan nodded. "He'll never lie to you. No matter how brutal, no matter how harsh, he'll never lie."

"What about school? I want to graduate." There had been a time when I hadn't cared if I'd finished school or not. In fact, I had preferred *not* to finish. But that had been a time when all I'd only wanted was my next high. I wasn't that girl anymore—no matter what everyone thought.

"You'll graduate, don't worry. In a few days, if not tomorrow, you'll be given an efficiency test. If you pass, you'll be allowed to graduate high school early. If not, you'll be required to study after your combat, weapons, and alien classes."

Great. If I failed the test, my workload would double. *If* I decided to stay.

Tests had never been easy for me. Frankly, I sucked at them. Five minutes after I would turn one in, I'd remember the answers I *should* have given.

"What if I want to go home?" I asked softly.

His lips lifted in a who-do-you-think-you're-kidding smile. "Please, Phoenix. Just please. After seeing what the Sybilins did, you'll never be able to go back to your normal life, doing nothing and knowing you could be doing something to make the world a safer place."

"First of all, don't assume you know me *or* what I can and can't do."

"I wasn't finished."

Eyes narrowed, I waved a hand through the air, a silent command for him to continue.

He tapped the end of my nose with his finger. "Sybilins make some alien breeds look like trained house pets. Believe me, there are much worse prowling our streets, stalking our families."

"Why haven't I heard about them then?"

"Like I said, we make sure the public doesn't know."

I didn't respond. I didn't know how to respond. What else was I ignorant about?

"Tell me you don't care about predatory species stalking your family. Tell me that doesn't bother you. Tell me you're happy doing nothing."

"Listen, I'll do or fight anything to keep my mother safe." Even though she'd sent me here, thinking the worst of me. A sharp pain of regret tore through me, but I ignored it. Fragile as she was, my mom would not be able to defend herself against predatory creatures. "But that doesn't mean I have to do that here. That doesn't mean this is the place for me. I like the idea of it, sure, but I'm just not—"

"Don't let Boss hear you talk like that," he snapped, cutting me off. "Kids all over the world would kill to be in your place and you're on shaky ground as it is."

"Maybe they would, and maybe I am." I scrubbed a hand down my face. "If I stay, will I be able to see my friends?"

"No." He didn't hesitate, didn't try to lie.

No.

With a half smile, he bumped my shoulder with his own. "It's not so bad, I promise. You'll make new friends."

He made it sound so easy, not the nerve-racking chore it was sure to be. That Kitten girl had been nice, I reminded myself, but she hadn't known about my past. She might run screaming the moment she did.

"I trained here," Ryan said, regaining my attention. "Now I teach here."

My eyes widened. "What do you teach?"

"Hand-to-hand combat." Once more he reached out, but this time he tweaked a strand of my hair instead of tapping my nose. Then he moved to brush the strand behind my ear. Before the action was complete, though, he stiffened. He dropped his arm to his side and cleared his throat. He backed two steps away. "This isn't a bad place to be. You might even come to love it."

What had *that* been about? Why had he moved away? Unsure about everything, I gazed down at my feet. Dirt dusted my boots, and splashes of dried beer stained the tops. "I just, I don't know," I admitted.

"Tell me what you don't know. I'll help you know."

I wished I could, but my mind was suddenly blank. Dark. So many emotions coursed through me that I couldn't name them all.

"Do you have a home to go back to, Phoenix?" he asked, showing no mercy.

I bit my bottom lip. My mom had truly washed her hands of me; there would be no going back to her. *She didn't even say good-bye.* God, how that still cut. Even my dad, pathetic coward that he was, had said good-bye.

If I returned, she'd just send me to another camp. And the next one could be a thousand times worse than this.

Here, at least, I would learn to fight, to defend myself and my world. *Can you kill?* I'd told them I could; I knew I could if necessary. But I didn't think I was ready to do it. Not really.

I shuddered to think of what that first death blow would be like. Still . . . "I'll stay," I said, my tone almost inaudible. I'd stay. For now. If, later, I decided to leave, I'd leave and nothing they said or did would stop me.

Slowly Ryan grinned. "I'm glad."

When he smiled at me like that, I was glad, too. I gulped, warm, tingling, suddenly needing to be touched. Kissed. I didn't understand my reaction to him, so I quickly changed the subject. "So, um, who were some of those people in there? Like the ballerina?"

"Ballerina?" He choked, his eyes nearly bugging out, and banged his chest with a fist. He cleared his throat. "You mean the dark-haired, violet-eyed babe?"

I nodded, not liking that he called the woman a babe.

His grin grew wider. "That's Mia Snow, the one who fought for you. Don't make her mad and don't let her hear you call her a ballerina. Something happened to her, I don't know what, that's eased some of the hate inside her, but she's still one of the most vicious, temperamental people I've ever met. She kills first and asks questions later."

And they let the woman around kids? Fabulous.

"The brown-haired woman with the hazel eyes is Le'Ace," Ryan said.

Ah, the perfect-looking one. The one with features so fine she could have walked straight from a priceless work of art.

"She's . . . I don't know if there's a word for what she is," Ryan told me. "She was genetically altered and is stronger, smarter, faster than anyone you've ever seen. She is emotion-less and will not disobey her commanders for any reason. If she's told to destroy someone, she destroys them. Age doesn't matter, gender doesn't matter. Background doesn't matter. They're simply dead."

"Is she even human?"

"No one's brave enough to ask her," he answered with a grin.

My eyes widened again. Dear Lord. It just got worse and worse. *These* were the people I was going to learn from? "What about the man who asked me all those questions? The one with silver hair and sunglasses?"

A dark blanket descended over Ryan's features, cutting off all sense of amusement. He appeared as emotionless as he claimed Le'Ace was. "That's Boss. He's been around a while and helped start A.I.R. He's in charge of everything and everyone here, and you do what he says, when he says it. No argument. The consequences for disobeying him are always harsh."

"And the redhead with the sweet voice?"

"That's Siren."

Perfect name, I thought. She had a bad personality, but I suspected her voice could convince people to do anything. "Is *she* human?"

"Yeah. Don't worry, though. You won't see much of her. She helps gather the new recruits and then disappears for a while. I don't know where."

Before I could respond, the door opened. A young girl was ushered inside the room by Roses. She had the weirdest hair I'd ever seen, with orange-gold stripes and brown and white hunks. Her eyes were up-tilted and golden, the irises pointed on top and bottom. Her skin was a pretty amber.

Roses somehow seemed taller and more muscled than I remembered. "Phoenix, meet Kitten," he said, "Kitten, meet Phoenix."

Kitten's lips curled in a welcoming smile, and I returned the greeting, no longer feeling quite so alone. She wasn't the ginormous musclegirl I'd envisioned. She was actually delicate and serene looking, like the other Terans I'd seen.

How had this creature fought an Ell Rollis and won?

"Nice to *see* you," she said.

"You, too." Why had an alien been chosen for an alien-fighting camp? Seemed weird to me. Wouldn't that mean she'd have to kill her own kind?

"Now I know everyone's name but yours," I said to Roses.

"I am Kadar." He leveled a hard gaze on Ryan. "Let's go, boy. Your father wants you back in the room."

His father?

I must have said the words aloud because Kadar said, "Boss. Top Brass, the big cheese."

My mouth fell open, and I glanced questioningly at Ryan.

He wasn't looking at me but at Kadar—who was in the process of turning on his heel and striding away, completely unconcerned. Ryan followed after him without a word. The moment he left the room, the door closed with a quiet whoosh.

His dad was the man in charge. I didn't know what to think of that.

"What the hell was that Q and A about?" Kitten burst out the moment we were alone. "They asked me the freakiest questions ever. Ev-er. My sister told me they'd interview me, but she didn't mention an all-out interrogation. They knew about every mistake I'd ever made."

"Me, too." Thankfully she didn't ask what my mistakes were. I explained what Ryan had told me, and Kitten's eyes—those lovely cat eyes of hers—titled higher. She actually purred.

"How long do you think we'll have to stay in this room?" she asked, rubbing her hands together. "I'm ready for action."

"I don't know." Also I didn't know why Boss failed to explain any of this to us. Did he *want* us left in the dark? If so, why? I mean, if the man's goal was to heap as much stress on us as possible, he'd already succeeded.

"I wonder how many kids are here and how they'll react to me," she said, the barest hint of vulnerability in her voice. "You know, 'cause I'm an Outer."

That she feared being rejected really resonated with me. If I hadn't liked her already, I would have then. "*I* like you," I said.

"Maybe we can be partners or something. But you better not let me down. I refuse to be one of the losers sent home."

She pranced around the small room, radiating excitement. She even rubbed her temples against the walls. "Just think. If we make it to the end of the program, we'll get to fight crime and all that shit. There's nothing better than kicking ass and taking names!"

I could think of a few things I liked better. Boys, music, *relaxing*.

"This is, without a doubt, the coolest thing to ever happen to me." As she spoke, her nails elongated to sharp points. The slight sheen of golden hair on her skin stood at attention.

I'd never been in a fight just for the fun of it. But I didn't have nine lives—did she?—so was going to be careful with the one I had. Finally.

"I wonder if we'll get to stay in barracks with the boys or not," she said.

"I don't know." What I wondered was if the instructors lived here. Say, a certain hand-to-hand combat instructor named Ryan. . . . Did he have a girlfriend? My hands tightened into fists at the thought.

"Uh, who are you thinking about, girl?" Kitten smiled over at me. "Your face got all gushy and red. And you better not say Bradley. I'd have to hurt you. That boy is a mhore and no friend of mine is going to date a mhore. Wait. We are going to be friends, right?"

"Yes." I blinked in confusion. "A what now?"

"A mhore. A male whore."

I barked out a laugh. "You don't have to worry about me

and Bradie boy. He's not my type." I hadn't dated in a while and had rarely dated boys my own age, but I didn't tell her that. I didn't want her to ask questions, like where I'd met my last boyfriend. Then I'd have to admit I'd been to rehab.

"So we're friends?" Kitten asked again.

"I hope so. I could use one right now."

"Me, too." She leaned close, whispering, "Who *were* you—"

The door opened for the third time, and the ballerina—Mia Snow, Ryan had called her—strode inside, holding a plastic cup. Kitten pressed her lips together and stared in awe.

Mia wore confidence like a cloak; it oozed from her. Despite that confidence, she didn't look capable of fighting me and actually winning. I was taller than she was by two inches.

However, she did look capable of killing me in cold blood. There was something about those enigmatic blue eyes that said, "Enjoy your current breath because it's your last."

Why had she fought for me? I didn't understand and was afraid to hope she saw something good in me. Yeah, she'd mentioned passion. But that didn't seem like enough to me.

"My name is Mia, and I'll be your guide." She stopped just in front of us and slapped the cup in my hand. "This is for you. I'm sure you already know the drill."

A blush heated my cheeks. My first drug test would be today, it seemed. Kitten stared at the cup in confusion.

So I wouldn't have to comment, I returned my attention to Mia, who was clad from neck to toe in skin-tight black syn-leather. At least, I thought it was syn-leather. I'd never seen material so soft and supple. Surely it wasn't real.

When the aliens had first came to our planet through inter-world portals and war had erupted, animals and plants had nearly been decimated. Some of our lakes had even dried up. We'd had to rebuild, well, everything—one of the reasons we were the "New World." Now we were a society who relied totally on synthetics—fakes, manufactured reproductions.

I didn't just know that from my history books. I knew that because of my great-grandpa. He'd lived through it and had delighted in telling me story after story of poverty and famine. During the rebuilding, the "Enlightened Age," he said they'd had to find new ways to survive and had relied on alien technology and alien food supplies.

"I'll be here for the next few weeks, helping you settle in," Mia continued. "If you're lucky, I'll even train you." Her voice was dainty, but like her eyes, it held layers of sharp steel. "If anyone bothers you or gives you trouble, don't come to me. Handle it yourself. That's part of being an agent." She paused, studied us. Whether she liked what she saw, I couldn't tell. "I believe a good team works together but a great team likes and respects each other. I can't make the others like you. *You* have to do that."

O-kay. That had just seriously lowered my chances.

"No questions? Good," she said before we had time to respond. "Let's do the tour thing. This way." She pivoted on her heel and seemed to float away.

Kitten and I shared a reeling glance, then trailed after her. I kept the cup at my side as a long, white hallway closed around us. What was it with these people and the color white?

This way, you'll stand out on the monitors, my common sense piped up.

Ahhh. Now that made sense.

"Did Bradley make it or was he rejected?" Kitten asked Mia, and I had to wonder about her obsession with the boy. Seemed like more than simple curiosity.

"For now, he's in," was Mia's response. "Who knows how long he'll be allowed to stay. He's been taken to the boy's quarters."

Kitten frowned. "No co-ed, huh. That would have rocked."

Mia cast a dark glance over her shoulder. "Fraternizing isn't forbidden, but it *is* discouraged. At least in the beginning. Neither of you need the distraction right now." Her gaze focused on me for a split second longer, hard and knowing.

I experienced a flash of resentment. She'd fought for me, but even she acted like the slightest thing would send me into a drug-induced tailspin.

I bet nothing distracted Agent Mia Snow, though. I stared at her. Long black hair swished over her back. The strands were like a midnight waterfall. Still, she looked like she was marching into battle. Ready to kill.

She made a sharp turn, and the walls became silver panels. "The floors are heat and weight sensitive; they logged you into the database the moment you stepped upon them. Your shoe size was taken, your measurements, and your retinal ID."

Wow. Talk about high-tech.

Talk about Big Brother. Constantly being watched was one of the reasons cameras had been outlawed without a license.

"This is a restricted area, and we'll know the moment you enter without permission," Mia said. "The computer will recognize your identity, and because of your measurements, it will know exactly how much of an electric shock to administer to hurt without killing."

I wasn't impressed by the technology anymore. I was pissed. "We're to be prisoners then?" I gritted out.

She shrugged, unconcerned. "It's for your protection."

"Oh, really. How so?" I insisted.

"There are other-worlders out there who want nothing more than to destroy this school and everyone inside it. If you were to sneak out, then inadvertently lead them back here . . . understand now?" she said.

My irritation drained, and I slowly nodded. Kitten did, too. If I decided to leave permanently, would they let me go without a fight? Dread slithered through me.

Two more turns and we came to a dead end. Mia placed her hand on one of the silver panels and a blue light flashed, consuming her arm to the elbow. At the same time, a red beam scanned her face.

"Welcome, Mia Snow," a computerized voice said.

The dead end split down the center, revealing a wide chasm that opened into a room far different from everything I'd seen of the camp up to that point. Bright colors. Furniture. Comfort. Like home.

Despite that, my palms began to sweat.

We entered a lounge area, and there was a smattering of girls. Some were watching a holoscreen, some were sitting at a table, snacking and talking, and some were strewn out on chairs and couches, reading. All of them stopped what they were doing and simply stared at me and Kitten. Conversations tapered to quiet.

Don't notice the cup, don't notice the cup. No one looked remotely friendly. No one said a word to us or even waved.

Kitten, I saw, was the only other-worlder in the group.

Mia kept a steady pace in front of us. "This area is known as the Common. You can relax and socialize here in your free time."

"You mentioned that we aren't allowed to leave the building," I said. "Does that mean we can't go outside at all?"

"Not for a while," Mia replied. "For the reason I mentioned before and because most of the world doesn't know about this program and that's the way we want to keep it. Once we know you can be trusted to keep the secret, even under torture, and once we know you are good enough to spot and lose a shadow, you will be allowed to leave at your leisure."

Forget the spotting and losing of a shadow. I had a feeling

it would take a long time to convince the agents to trust me with their secrets. Not only that, but torture? The only way to prove I could keep a secret while being tortured was to actually be tortured and keep the secret. A shudder raked my spine.

We exited the Common and entered a forked foyer. The walls were painted a pretty shade of blue, but there were no holoimages, no pictures.

Mia turned left. "Your room is this way," she said. "I hope you're memorizing the path."

Uh, no. I hadn't been. There were a few girls in this hallway, and they mashed themselves against the wall as Mia passed them.

"Everyone has a roommate," she continued. "There is to be no fighting in your room. Save it for the combat arena."

Rolling her eyes, Kitten raised her fist up and down in front of her chest, mimicking a guy masturbating.

"I see that, girl," Mia said without turning around.

Kitten paled and her mouth fell open. I cut off a laugh.

Mia stopped at an arched doorway at the very end of the hall. She faced us, her expression blank. "This is your room. Kitten, place your palm in the center of the black box."

I peeked around Mia's head to see what black box she was talking about. It was at the side of the door, a perfect square at eye level. Multicolored buttons lined the top.

Tentatively Kitten reached out and did as she'd been told. A blue light similar to the one that had scanned Mia's hand traced the entire surface of Kitten's palm. "It's warm," Kitten said.

"Scan complete," a computer-animated voice said. "Welcome, Kitten."

Blinking in surprise, Kitten dropped her arm to her side. Mia flicked me a glance. "Your turn, Phoenix."

Once my scan was finished, Mia punched a series of button and the door opened. "Besides the staff, only the two of you will be able to enter this room." She paused for several seconds, head tilting to the side as if in thought. "Unless, of course, some of the girls have finally mastered breaking and entering, then it's open season. I suggest you study ways to increase security."

Shock coursed through me. "We'll learn how to break into people's homes?"

"Of course," she said, her tone suggesting I was silly for even asking. "Not all of your targets will surrender easily. They'll hide. They'll lock themselves away. You'll have to be able to reach them no matter where they are, won't you?"

"Yes," I said, excited by the thought. It was just so . . . *bad,* yet would be totally legal when doing it as an agent. Too cool.

"Hell yeah," Kitten said.

Slowly Mia grinned. I guess she liked our enthusiasm. "I suggest you study the map inside your manual, as well. I will not be giving you a tour of the rest of the building. You'll be expected to learn and memorize the layout on your own be-

101

cause you'll be expected to memorize the cities you enter and the prey you stalk on your own." She didn't wait for our response, but strode into my new room.

Curious about the place I would now call home, I followed quickly. It was small but clean, with two stiff-looking beds, two plain, silver dressers, two silver desks, and a bathroom with a toilet, mirror, and dry-enzyme shower stall.

"There are clothes for each of you in the dresser. Standard uniform of white pants and top."

"Yipp-eeee," Kitten muttered. "Uniforms."

"You may write your family, but be advised that all correspondence will be monitored." She spread her arms wide. "If you have any questions, there is a manual inside the top left drawer of your desk. I suggest you read it. Memorize it."

"Sure thing," I said.

She turned to Kitten. "You're going to spend the next two minutes sprinting in the hall."

"Wait. What? I—"

"Go!" Mia snapped.

Kitten leapt into action, running into the hallway.

Now Mia looked to me. "I suggest you fill the cup. I've bought you two minutes. Whether you're done or not—"

I didn't hear the rest. I was racing into the bathroom. As quickly as I could, I filled and capped the cup, righted my clothing, and strode back into the room. Mia was wearing gloves, I noticed. She took the cup, her gaze locked on mine.

"You'd better not let me down."

"I won't." I hoped.

Panting, Kitten raced back into the room. "All . . . done." She hunched over, anchoring her elbows on her knees. "What was that for?"

"Question me again and you'll run for an hour straight. See you around, girls." Mia strode from the room, the door shutting behind her.

"What have we gotten ourselves into?" I breathed.

"I'm not sure yet." Kitten fell onto one of the beds. "If I figure it out, I'll let you know."

7

Page one of the A.I.R. Trainee manual

Dear A.I.R. trainee,
Half of you will be sent home before the end of
the first month, your memories wiped. Another
half will be sent home the second month. For
now, you're here. Forget everything you've heard
about A.I.R. Forget every "self-defense" move
you've learned. Basically, forget everything the
outside world has taught you. It means nothing
here. Less than nothing, actually, because what
you think you know will get you killed in this
new world.

The *real* world.

Does that scare you? If not, you're stupid. You

don't yet have the necessary skills to protect yourself from the elusive enemy that walks—and
hunts—among us. Hopefully by the end of this
year-long training program you will. Here you
will fight with your hands, with your mind, with
every weapon imaginable, and even some that
aren't.

You will become a deadly weapon.

Will you be allowed to kill and strike indis-
criminately? No. An A.I.R. agent's job is to find
and stop the aliens who are predatory, destructive. But only those. The rest you will leave
alone.

A.I.R. was formed to protect humans. That,
more than anything, is our job.

You were chosen for this program because you
have demonstrated potential, bravery, and the
right temperament. Which means the rest of the
world already finds you too wild, too undisci-
plined, and too violent.

Even though we admire those qualities, do
not make the mistake of thinking you will be un-
fettered here. You'll endure more rules and regula-
tions than ever before—and you *will* obey them,
probably for the first time in your life. If not, you
will be punished severely.

Pray you never find out what I mean by that.

Let us begin with a few of the above-mentioned rules.

1. Do not attempt to leave the building without permission.

2. Girls do not enter the boys' barracks and boys do not enter the girls'. No exceptions.

3. Relationships between trainees and trainers are prohibited. You are legally an adult, yes, but you will not date or have any type of sexual relationship with the instructors.

4. Do not use drugs. This includes: Onadyn in all its incarnations: Snow Angels, Breathless, Nose Candy, Puffs, and Flyers. All forms of cocaine, the White Pony, Whiz, Liquid Gold, Rush, Iron Brew, Jellies, Vallies, Chronic, Dragon Rocks, Doves, X, marijuana, or any other upper, dower, mixed, blended powder, liquid, or puffer not mentioned that will impair your judgment in any way. If you get sick, go to the clinic here. Do not self-medicate.

5. Do not be late to class for any reason.

We operate on a strike-three basis. Break one rule, you will be punished—severely as I mentioned above. Break two rules, you will be punished. Once again, the punishment will be severe. But if you break three rules, your memory will be wiped and you will be returned home.

And know this, if you break a rule you *will* be caught. My eyes are everywhere.

Good luck and welcome.

Boss

Page two

The map. (Or rather, maze.) Building after building, all connected through intricate hallways and more hallways. There were classrooms, barracks for both boys and girls, two Commons, many restricted areas, a gym, a weapons room, an interrogation room (just the thought made my stomach hurt), and an observation room.

Page three

Things to do in your spare time:

Exercise. Stamina is important.

Study your notes from class. A sharp mind is important.

Practice handling your pyre-gun. A steady hand is important. Be careful not to shoot your teammates.

Practice sparring. Being able to take down an opponent is important.

I pinched the bridge of my nose. Those were the things we should do with our spare time? Interesting that they didn't mention slapping each other around or knifing each other while we slept. Hurting and killing were *important*. Right?

Groaning, I flipped the page.

Page four

Classes you will attend over the next year:
Alien anatomy
Alien biology
Weapons of the world—and otherworlds
Combat
Alien history and sociology
Breaking and entering
The art of stalking
Alien races and relations
Global governments
Interrogation
Computer sciences

With a weary sigh, I put the manual aside and lay down. "Lights out," I muttered. Instantly the light on my side of the room dimmed, throwing the room into pitch black. Most of the day had wasted away, anyway, and Kitten was already asleep. She and I had talked for hours, getting to know each other better. The more I learned about her, the more I liked.

She was playful, witty, and loyal. She came from a big family and I could see the affection in her eyes every time she mentioned her sisters and brothers. If they needed her, she'd do anything and everything to get to them.

I was a little envious. I'd always wanted a sister, but my mom hadn't remarried or even dated since my dad left. She worked and took care of me, and that was about it. Maybe my dad had had another kid with his new wife. I could very well have a sister or brother I didn't know about. Since leaving us, he hadn't even called.

A sharp pain tore through me with the thought.

Just go to sleep. For the next few hours, I tossed and turned, unable to settle. I was wearing unfamiliar clothes, stiff and a little snug. The mattress was firmer than mine at home, and the blanket lacked the fresh smell I was used to. The room was too dark, the only hint of light coming from the wall clock. I could hear Kitten's soft exhalations and purrs.

My mind raced as pieces of the "welcome" letter in the manual continually took center stage. If I broke three rules, my memory would be wiped. How much of my memory, though? Everything or just camp? Everything might not be such a bad thing. I thought I might like starting from scratch, with nothing of the past to taint my thoughts.

Still. I hadn't known something like that was possible.

I'd decided to stay here for now. But I didn't like rules—never had—and didn't like the thought of being so constrained. And so . . . *punished* if I failed.

I expelled a deep sigh and forced myself to think of anything other than A.I.R. Of course, my mom was the first thing that popped into my head. What was she dreaming of just then? Did she even miss me?

When I was a little girl, she'd held me close and sung me to sleep every night. She'd baked me breakfast every morning, smiling all the while. She'd been so happy. So carefree. Then my dad had left. Then I started doing drugs. All her happiness seemed to vanish. All the cares of the world seemed to settle on her shoulders.

At least I'd had Jamie to lean on, as bad an influence as she'd been. My mom had had no one when she should have had me.

God, I owed her so much. Tears burned my eyes.

Okay. Now I couldn't think about her, either.

Think about Ryan . . . his sexy image sprang into my mind, making me shiver. Relationships between trainer and trainee were forbidden, the manual had said, but that didn't stop me from hoping he found me half as attractive as I found him. I would have liked to kiss him. Just once. With tongue, his arms—

Suddenly all the lights in the room flashed on, extremely bright to my eyes, which had become attuned to the dark. The beige walls came into focus, the metallic dresser. A mirror. I saw my reflection: rumpled, long blond hair. Sleep-heavy brown eyes. Swollen lips. I'd chewed them the entire time I'd lain awake, I guess, not realizing I was doing it.

"Kitten and Phoenix," a computerized voice said.

Kitten jolted upright, her gaze wild as she looked around. "What happened? What's wrong?" Her voice was scratchy.

"Your presence is required in room three A. You have ten minutes," the computer finished.

Groaning, I eased up and rubbed a hand over my face. "I wonder what they're going to do to us."

"Or what they'll make us do," Kitten grumbled. She threw her legs over the side of her bed. "What time is it?"

I glanced at the digital clock and its flashing red numbers. "Three a.m."

"What?" She frowned. "You're kidding."

"Look for yourself."

She did. Her frown deepened. "That's insanity! Who gets up at three a.m.?"

"Apparently we do." I lumbered out of bed. We took turns in the dry shower, the enzyme spray cleaning us in seconds. We hurriedly brushed our teeth and hair before studying the mazelike map in the manual.

"We should have studied this more carefully before bed," she mumbled.

"Note to self," I said. "Listen to Mia Snow when she speaks."

"Three A," Kitten said, tapping a long, pointed nail on her chin. "Looks like that's like four halls over. We'll never make it in time."

"Crap. We can't break a rule on our first day."

"Well, we've only got three minutes."

"Then let's haul ass!" Determination filled me. "Come on." I raced to the door and commanded it to open.

"What will the assholes who run this place do if we get lost?" Kitten said behind me. "Choke us with our own intestines?"

I didn't want to find out. "Being late is probably worse than committing murder."

"We'll never make it," she repeated.

"Yes, we will."

We rushed into the hall and maneuvered through the unfamiliar passage. As we ran, Kitten fastened her multicolored hair into a ponytail.

Unlike the walls in the interview room, these hall walls were blue with posters taped throughout. THE FEW, THE PROUD, AND THE BADASS, one of them read. IT'S NOT HOW YOU DO IT, IT'S THE END RESULT THAT COUNTS, another said.

Surprisingly, there were other girls in the hallways, hustling from one room to another. No one said a word to us or even glanced in our direction. They were too focused, too hurried to reach their own destination.

Finally we found a door that had a large black 3A over the top. After a quick hand scan, we were able to enter. Mia Snow stood at the head of the room, her arms locked behind her back.

"You're late," she said. "And that's not a good way to start the program. You're lucky I don't kick you out right now."

"We're not late," I told her through clenched teeth, trying not to pant. "It's three ten."

Her dark brows arched. "If someone is six seconds late, they are . . . what?"

"Late," Kitten and I muttered together.

"I told you to study the map."

"We did," Kitten said. "Kind of."

I had glanced at it last night, but I hadn't tried to memorize it. *Too complicated,* I'd thought. I wouldn't make that mistake again. I *would* learn.

Mia's response was a commanding, "On the floor. Now!"

I looked at Kitten, and she looked at me. On the floor? Seriously?

"I didn't say stare at each other." There was violence in Mia's tone. "I said drop."

We dropped.

A minute passed in silence before Mia said anything else. She glanced down at her nails, suddenly radiating a breezy air. "I'm feeling magnanimous today. I'm going to watch you do twenty-five push-ups, twenty-five sit-ups, and twenty-five knee bends. Start."

"Are you kidding me?" Kitten gasped out.

"Make that fifty." Mia arched a brow. "Anything else you'd like to say?"

The words "help me" and "oh my God" came to mind. I remained quiet, though, and forced myself into motion. By the time I finished, I was a sweaty, burning, shaking mess. I'd never done so much exercise in my life. Kitten breezed through it as if she'd worked out her entire life.

I was beyond jealous.

"You're slow, Phoenix, and I expect improvement next time."

Next time? I barely cut off my moan. "I'll do better."

"Make sure of it," was her clipped response. "By the way, you passed the test."

A pause. "What test?" Kitten asked.

"I wasn't talking to you," Mia snapped.

No, she'd been talking to me. I'd passed the drug test. Thank God.

"Make sure you pass the next one, as well, or I will be very upset."

I gulped and nodded, not glancing in Kitten's direction.

"Sit, both of you." Even issuing orders in the middle of the night, Mia was still as pretty as a ballerina. Her hair gleamed darkly in the light, like black silk. Her face was smooth, her eyes bright. Did the woman not need to sleep?

Both Kitten and I sat on the floor, right where we were. I sent my gaze throughout the room. It was like every classroom I'd ever been inside and that surprised me. I guess I'd expected guns and knives to be hanging on the walls. A mat for fighting, maybe. Not math equations projected from holoscreens. Not desks and chairs.

"At a desk, girls," Mia said with a roll of her eyes.

Kitten and I scurried to the desks at the head of the class and sat like good little frightened robots.

"Now, then. Welcome to orientation." Mia sounded calm and emotionless once again. She locked her hands behind her back. "I bet you're wondering why you were called out of bed this early in the morning on your first day here." She paced in front of us.

I nodded. Kitten did, as well. Neither one of us spoke. It wasn't that I was intimidated by Mia—okay, I was—but because I was awed by her. She was fluid and graceful, lithe, as she moved. What's more, she was lethal in a way I hadn't realized before. Every few seconds, she dropped her hands to her side and fingered the hilt of a blade strapped to her waist.

"You're here at this hour because most A.I.R. agents work at night. Yes, some work during the day, just like cops, because law is needed even in the daylight. But our sun is too strong and too damaging for a lot of otherworlders, so most crimes happen at night. You need to learn to embrace this hour."

I nodded again, even though a part of me wanted to leave the room. Sure I was fascinated by what she was saying—I hadn't known aliens were sensitive to our sunlight—but I resented being taught this way, as if we needed permission to take our next breath.

Kindness wouldn't have killed her.

"While your regular classes will begin later today, you will first watch videos of alien crimes. You will watch how A.I.R.

agents successfully—and at times, unsuccessfully—hunted and fought their targets. Watch closely. Learn."

"Have you killed?" I asked, finding my voice.

She nodded without hesitation. "Many times."

"Do you regret it?"

Again, she didn't hesitate. "I don't regret a single action I've taken. It will be best for you if you come to terms with what you must do now rather than later. Emotions will weaken you. They will distract you." She shoved back the sleeve of her shirt, revealing the length of her arm.

The first thing I noticed was a tattoo of the Grim Reaper's scythe. It stretched across her arm from wrist to elbow, a black talisman. The second thing I noticed was the long, puckered scar that slashed beside it.

"Ooohh," Kitten breathed.

"Predatory other-worlders," Mia said, "will not hesitate to kill you. Or your family. Do not hesitate to kill them first." She dropped the sleeve and lifted a remote from the granite counter behind her, then pressed a button. Images began flashing over the far holoscreen.

Violent images. Bloody images. People fighting creatures I'd never seen before, in ways I'd never seen before. My mouth dropped open. It was a lethal dance of blades and guns and fists. Of teeth and claws and fury.

Of crimson blood, of black blood.

A couple of times I heard Kitten gasp. I glanced over at her, if only to escape the screen for a moment. Her face was pale. She'd been so happy at the prospect of fighting only a few hours earlier. Probably before she realized that death would come of it. Maybe hers.

I wasn't horrified like I probably should have been. Scared, yeah. That, I had in spades. Who wouldn't, with new knowledge of alien powers—mind control, walking through walls, teleporting. Not to mention the guns and knives, claws and teeth.

Like I'd told Ryan, I was willing to do anything to protect my mom from these *things*. I wanted, finally, to be a girl she could be proud of. I wanted to make up for all the times I'd told her that her job as a waitress was meaningless and that what she did for me wasn't enough. I'd only ever caused havoc and emotional pain to those around me. If I decided to see this A.I.R. thing through, could finally change that. Excitement bubbled inside me at the thought. For once, I could be a hero.

Doubts, though, were excitement crushers. What if I was one of the ones kicked out after the first month? No one but Mia had wanted me in the first place. I mean, really. Should I put all my energy into something that would most likely be taken from me?

I just didn't know.

Suddenly the woman named Siren, the one with the sweet voice, came onto the screen, capturing my full attention. She walked toward a group of other-worlders, humming under her breath as if she hadn't a care. The pale-skinned, pale-haired creatures were smiling as if they were entranced. When she reached them, she went silent, jumped up, higher and faster than I'd ever seen anyone move, and she attacked with a single knife.

They were dead in seconds.

Then Mia's beautiful face came onto the screen. It was night and she stalked toward a giant, muscled man with yellow scales instead of skin. He did not have a nose. *Ah, an Ell Rollis,* I thought, recalling the description Kitten had given me. The Outer had a little boy by the throat and was squeezing. The boy was flailing.

Mia approached them silently. When she reached them, she raised a knife. It glinted silver in the moonlight. Without a word, she reached around the monster and slit its throat. Just like that. One minute he was alive, the next he wasn't.

Kitten gasped again as the giant tumbled to a bloody heap, releasing the boy along the way. I never got to find out what happened to that little boy because the screen went blank.

Real-life Mia stepped in front of the screen. For a long while, she didn't speak. She regarded us intently, studying. Then, slicing through the silence as deftly as she'd sliced the alien, she said, "Think you can handle this life?"

Could I?

Kitten gave an uncertain nod.

"Yes," I said, suddenly knowing it beyond any doubt. I could. The real question was, would A.I.R. let me?

8

We spent two more hours in orientation, going through some tests to determine if we had the smarts to graduate high school early or needed more classes and exactly what level of instruction we'd require. Of course, we weren't told our grade. We had to wait for that.

Afterward, Mia escorted us to our next class. The room was an exact replica of the other—except this one had other girls inside. My nervous system kicked into gear, as if it was the first day of high school all over again. Would they like me? Would they instantly hate me? How long had they been a part of the school?

Would I cause my brain to bleed by asking myself too many questions?

"Everyone, I need your attention. I'd like you to meet Kitten." Mia urged Kitten forward with an insistent push. "And this is Phoenix." She shoved me forward, as well.

I stumbled to a stop and gave a little wave. "Hey."

"Hey," I heard from several of them. Some of my nervousness eased. Obviously they didn't plan to ignore me.

"This is Alien Anatomy 101," Mia said. "Mishka Le'Ace will be your instructor. Everyone calls her Le'Ace."

I didn't mean to, but I yawned. I was not used to lack of sleep.

Mia's eyes narrowed on me. "Am I boring you, Miss Germaine?"

My cheeks heated as everyone's attention focused on me. "No."

"You're boring *me*," a clipped voice said.

From the corner of my eye, I saw a woman step forward. I turned and faced her, immediately seeing it was the beauty from yesterday's interview, the one with the most exquisite, perfect features of any human I'd ever seen. Probably in the entire world.

"She's genetically altered," Ryan had said.

Up close, her rich brown hair was glossier than I'd realized, her hazel eyes sparked with green, and her lips glistened with the perfect amount of gloss. Her skin was flawless. She wore a red dress suit, perfectly tailored to fit her perfect curves.

I wanted to hate her, but she looked too much like an angel.

Ryan had told me she was emotionless, born to kill anyone and anything when ordered. If I'd have met her on the streets, I never would have guessed. I would have thought she was a model or a businesswoman. Maybe that was why she was so good at her job. Who would expect her to render a death blow?

She probably walked up to her targets, smiled sweetly, and then killed them before they realized what was going on.

"Thank you, Miss Snow," Le'Ace said in that formal voice of hers. She had a crisp accent I couldn't quite place. Russian, maybe. "I can take it from here."

Mia strode out of the room.

I moved toward one of the empty desks, but Le'Ace stopped me. "Not yet, Phoenix. First, I have a test for you."

Frowning, I froze in place. The new teacher was picking on me already, it seemed.

Kitten tried to move around me.

"Nope. You too, Kitten. Turn around and face the wall," Le'Ace said, showing no mercy.

Several seconds passed, and we did nothing. Just remained in place. What kind of test was she going to give us that we needed to turn around and face the wall? Did she plan to whip us to see how much we could tolerate? Strike us from behind? Or was turning around the actual test? Maybe we were supposed to know that to turn our back to her was to give her power over us.

Damn, but this was confusing. I envisioned myself making the wrong choice and getting myself kicked out *today*.

"Turn. Around," Le'Ace commanded sharply. Obviously she was not used to being disobeyed.

Apprehension and a little resentment slithered through me, to be treated like a child again. My jaw popped as I finally pivoted on my heel. Now was not the time to rebel. Kitten quickly followed suit.

"Good," Le'Ace said. She walked to us, her red heels clicking against the tile. "You're going to tell me everything you remember about the room and its occupants. Every detail. Phoenix, you're first. Tell me about the girls."

I breathed a sigh of relief. So, turning around hadn't been the test. I only had to—ah, crap. Did I even remember a single detail about the girls? I'd been so nervous, I hadn't really looked at them. "I don't remember."

"You must remember something." My back was to her, but I could feel the condemnation radiating from her. "Concentrate," she barked, sounding like a military general. "Think."

I closed my eyes and blanked my mind. Concentrating as she'd commanded, I replayed my entry, trying to soak in every detail. I saw . . . nothing.

"You will not have this long in the field," Le'Ace said. "If this were a mission, you'd be dead by now."

Several girls snickered. My cheeks heated for the second time.

"Tell me what you see," she ordered.

Think. You have to remember something. "There are eight girls sitting at the desks, and they're wearing white clothes.

Just like me." How was that for stating the obvious and trying to buy myself some time? "Two are black." *Yes!* I thought with satisfaction. That was right, I knew it was.

Suddenly a picture of them formed in my mind, details I thought I'd overlooked as clear as if I was actually looking at them. "One of the girls is Asian. One, the one with white hair, has a tattoo on her face." I was so proud of myself, I wanted to clap.

"And what is the tattoo?" came the unimpressed response.

My shoulders tensed as I focused on the girl in my mind. I mentally brushed away the white strands of hair shielding her cheek, revealing more and more of her face . . . the marking . . . "It's blue." And it had sweeping . . . no. Wrong. What was that? "The edges are jagged but . . . I can't see it clearly," I admitted.

"Yes, you can. Think harder." Le'Ace patted me on the back and it was a surprisingly rough *thump, thump.* More strength than I would have deemed such a beauty capable of displaying.

My hands clenched at my sides, and I squeezed my eyelids as tight as I could. I pictured the white-haired girl again. Her desk was in the third row. Her hair was long and straight and—oh! She had blue streaks in her hair. Streaks that matched the color of the tattoo. I told Le'Ace.

"That's right," she said, "but that's not what I wanted to know."

Obviously the woman was a task master. *Concentrate!* Tattoo. Blue. Pointed ends. Three pointed ends, to be exact. My eyes blinked open as the answer slammed into me. "It's a trident," I said, confident.

"Good. Slow, but good." Le'Ace patted my back again, and this blow almost hammered me to the floor. She must not know her own strength. Or maybe she did and just didn't care. "Remember to study a room and its occupants every time you walk into someplace new.

Her approval warmed me, and I found myself grinning.

"Kitten," she said, "it's your turn. Tell me about the room itself."

I twisted so that I could see the girls I'd just spoken about. They were exactly as I'd pictured them, even though I'd only had a few glances. Pride filled me. In the past, I'd studied my surroundings to make sure there were no cops present so I could fly. This time, I'd done it for a good reason.

My teachers used to tell me I'd killed so many brain cells by doing Onadyn that I'd never be sharp, never be considered intelligent. Those comments had hurt, still hurt, actually, when I allowed myself to think of them. I liked to think they'd told me those things to make me stop doing drugs, not because they thought I was stupid.

"The walls are light brown," Kitten began.

When she said no more, Le'Ace said, "Is that the only color?"

There was a long pause. I crossed my fingers behind my back. *You can do it, Kitten.*

"Yes?" Kitten said, though the word emerged as a question.

"Are you sure?"

"No. Yes. Yes, I'm sure."

"Good. But do not let someone's question waver you and do not give an answer unless you are sure. Now, what else do you remember? You've had plenty of time to think about it."

"There's a holoscreen above the center platform and the floor is made from silver tiles."

"You can see the floor now," Le'Ace said dryly. "That doesn't count. What about the desks? The chairs? How many are there?"

"I don't know," Kitten replied, and her voice was tortured.

"Think."

"I am!" she hissed.

"Think," Le'Ace said in that still, crisp voice.

Another pause.

Kitten shrugged. "Twenty?"

Le'Ace pushed out a breath. "Wrong. Turn around and count. If these desks had been aliens, you would be dead."

Seemed we'd be dead from a lot of things if this was the real world.

Kitten turned, and her cheeks were flushed a rosy red. "Twenty-one." She stomped her foot. "I was close!"

"Close will not keep you alive. Close will send you to an early grave."

Kitten's shoulders sagged. "I'll do better next time."

"I hope so. Even if you had said twenty-one, you would have been guessing and that is simply not good enough. I told you not to guess. Details are important. Every detail. A single detail can save your life or destroy it. You must be aware of everything at all times."

"Impossible," I said. What she was saying was impossible. No way a person could input so many details so quickly.

"You had your fingers crossed at one point." She arched a perfectly sculpted brow. "I know that but I wasn't looking at you."

I pressed my lips together and tried not to be impressed.

"But you are," she said as if she'd read my mind. Maybe she had. Was that possible? I gulped. More and more I was learning just how little I knew about the world and its inhabitants. "Have a seat, girls. Take a few minutes to meet the others."

"But she's an alien," a blonde said, pointing to Kitten. "I don't want to get to know her."

Kitten hissed.

Le'Ace frowned. "She's nonpredatory. You'll treat her as you treat the other students or you'll return home. Understand? If you don't, you can go to your room and pack your bags right now."

Everyone nodded, which saved them from my wrath. Right now, Kitten was my only friend. I was feeling a little protective of her.

I walked to the seat in back, between the tattooed blonde and the lovely Asian girl.

"Hey," the Asian said.

"Hey," I replied.

Tattoo turned away from me, giving me her profile. Asian leaned toward me and whispered loud enough for everyone to hear, "I'm Cara. Pay no attention to Emma, the bitch beside you. She hates everyone."

Emma didn't respond to the jab.

"I'm Johanna," one of the blond girls said, the one who had spoken against Kitten. "I saw you enter the Common yesterday. You don't look as nervous today."

"Well, I've since read that oh so comforting manual," I said dryly.

All the girls laughed. Except for Emma, whose gaze remained straight ahead. Still, I found myself relaxing. For the most part, they seemed to like me. How long would that last?

"Hey, Phoenix," Kitten called. She'd taken an open seat up front. "This is Dani, Lindsay, and Jenn." She motioned to a pretty blonde, a redhead, and the second black girl.

The girls smiled at me, and I returned the greeting.

"*They're* nice," Kitten added with a pointed look at Johanna.

"Hey, I'm nice," Johanna said. "Your heritage just caught me off guard, okay? We're supposed to kill Outers, not befriend them."

"Not all aliens are bad," Kitten growled.

Johanna held up her hands, palms out. "I believe you, all right? God. Give me a freaking break. I haven't slept in, like, a week."

"Why don't you two start over?" I suggested.

Both nodded reluctantly. I introduced Kitten to the girls I'd met, and they exchanged greetings.

"All right," Le'Ace said. She stood at the head of the class, her arms anchored behind her back. "Now that everyone knows everyone else, let's get started."

Was it bad that I already wanted a break?

"This is Alien Anatomy 101. I will teach you everything A.I.R. knows about aliens and their bodies. As a bonus, I will teach you about their powers, their abilities, and their weaknesses. Some we know for sure, some are just guesses." She leaned her hip against the metal counter. "What you learn in here needs to be applied in all of your weapons and combat classes."

I settled more comfortably into my seat and cast another glance at Kitten. She was listening raptly, as if the world could be conquered with Le'Ace's words alone. Maybe it could. Kitten was also licking her hand and purring. Weird, but cute.

"At your desks, each of you has a computerized notebook."

I looked down at my desk, but saw nothing. Wait. There was the faint outline of a silver box. But it was not raised and seemed to be part of the desk.

"Place your hands on it," Le'Ace instructed.

I did, and the moment my hands touched the silver, a virtual screen appeared, as did the shadow of a keyboard.

"The computer recognizes your fingerprints. As you type, the pages will be printed in your room."

Okay. That was seriously cool.

"Let's begin with lesson number one. This," Le'Ace said, "is an Arcadian." The moment she spoke the alien name, an image appeared on the holoscreen behind her. A tall, white-haired, violet-eyed male stared down at us. He was beautiful. Mesmerizing. Powerful. Savage. Raw. I wanted to stare at him forever.

"He's also Mia Snow's boyfriend, so do not lust too much," Le'Ace added, and there was genuine amusement in her tone. Not so emotionless after all.

"I thought dating aliens was against the law," Jenn said, her dark eyes roving over the other students.

Especially for an agent. Right?

Le'Ace shrugged. "Most assume it is against the law. That is what the government wants you to think. Once it was, but now it is merely frowned upon. There is a punishment, though. Civilians will look upon you with disdain. But Mia is not someone who cares about that." She eyed us, one by one. "The lesson here is that you must be prepared for the consequences if you decide to break any type of directive."

I had so many questions about Mia and the alien, but

Le'Ace continued the lecture. "I will occasionally bring an alien ally here for you to question. There is a Raka, a golden one, named Eden Black, who has killed more aliens than even Mia. Her insight is invaluable. There is a Targon, the strongest warriors to invade our planet, who has promised to visit. His name is Devyn and his telekinetic powers are vast."

I couldn't wait to meet them and see them in action.

Le'Ace continued, "Enough about what is to come. Let us concentrate on today's lesson. While the Arcadians have bodies and internal organs very similar to ours, they possess many abilities, most of which originate in the mind. Some are psychic. Some are mind readers. Some can control your thoughts and actions."

"How are we to guard ourselves from that?" I asked before I could stop myself. I didn't know proper procedure for questioning the teacher here. At my old school, I would have been sent to the office for speaking up without permission.

"I'll teach you," she answered as if I'd done nothing wrong. "When the time comes."

For several hours, she lectured about the Arcadians, about their overcrowded planet, and their genetic makeup, so different from ours.

I absorbed it all, typing constantly—and praying there weren't too many typos. It was fascinating.

"All right, girls," Le'Ace said. "I've told you about the Arcadian body. Now I want you to apply what you learned.

Go." She waved a hand toward the door. "Ryan awaits you in the cage."

Ryan?

My pulse thundered to a gallop. Whatever "the cage" was, I didn't care. I was just happy to get to see Ryan again.

9

We rode an elevator to the basement, each of us silent and unsure. To distract myself—Ryan!—I finally piped up with, "Has anyone been to the cage before?"

A chorus of "no" filled the small enclosure.

"I don't know about the rest of you, but I can't wait to see Ryan again," Dani said with a wicked grin. "That boy is hot!"

Murmurs of agreement circled, and I fought a wave of jealousy. A part of me considered him mine. My property. *I* had a crush on him, which meant I wanted him to be hands-off to the other girls. So what that he was forbidden to date me? So what that he might not feel the same about me?

He was cute. He was (sometimes) sweet.

"Oh, cool," Jenn said. "Look."

I followed the direction in which she pointed. There were multicolored buttons on the side wall and there was a screen on the back wall that flashed images of Arcadians fighting humans.

A preview of our next class, perhaps?

"Word on the street is you've fought side-by-side with him, Phoenix," Jenn said. "What's he like?"

I didn't have to ask who "he" was.

Dani's eyes widened. "You fought with him?"

"Yes," I answered, "and he's okay." I didn't want to increase their salivating.

"Okay?" Cara nudged my arm. "That's all? Come on. Surely there's more."

"Nope. That really is all." Except maybe, *he's mine*. And, *don't touch*.

When did you become so possessive?

Since last night, when he'd invaded my thoughts and all I wanted to do was kiss him.

"I wonder what we'll have to do in the cage," I said, taking us back to the subject that had started all the wonderings about Ryan. Would we be locked up? Forced to fight each other? I chewed on my bottom lip, wondering how *that* would go over.

Boys could fight and make up, no problem. Girls couldn't. None that I'd met, at least. Girls held grudges for every scratch.

"I hate that we're forbidden to date the instructors," Cara whined, disregarding my subject change. "I'm already imagining the things I could do to Ryan. . . ."

Grrr. My teeth gnashed together. Maybe fighting in the cage wasn't such a bad idea. Cara could use an introduction to my fist.

All this anger over a boy who probably doesn't remember your name?

He'd remember, I thought, chin lifting. He'd even tweaked my nose. *Actions of a brother to a sister, idiot.*

"If top brass is going to have a nondating rule like that," Kitten purred, "then the instructors need to be ugly."

Everyone laughed. Even me. She was right. So far, every instructor I'd seen was a candidate for a beefcake or angelcake holocalendar. I guess I understood the need for a certain body type, though. To catch predators, you had to be fast. You had to be strong. You had to be flexible.

I wasn't particularly fast. Or flexible. Yet. But I would be, I vowed. I'd work hard. I'd exercise. I'd—gag—eat right. Maybe Ryan would notice me as more than a sister type then.

"What kind of meals do they serve here?" I asked. More important, when was breakfast? If the food was anything like what I'd endured at rehab, I was going to suffer. Small portions, bland, and gross.

Before anyone could answer, the elevator doors glided open and the light inside it dimmed. All sense of amusement faded from our group as darkness enveloped us.

"What is this place?" Kitten whispered.

"I can't see anything," Johanna said, unsure. "Can you see? Can anyone see?"

"It's like a black hole," Lindsay breathed.

Like the others, I couldn't see anything but gloom and shadow.

"Do we enter?" Dani asked quietly.

"We might as well." A little nervous, I took the lead and moved forward. I kept my arms outstretched, trying not to bump into anything. I encountered a wall and turned away from it. "This is probably a test."

"Maybe we're supposed to stay in the elevator to pass," Jenn said with a shaky lilt.

"Maybe that's the perfect way to fail." I hit another wall and cursed under my breath. "We're in this together. We'll be fine." A moment passed and none of them moved. Or rather, I didn't hear any of them move.

"All right," Kitten said. "Let's do this."

I felt her inch up behind me, latch onto my arm, and we moved forward together. I tripped once, twice, but kept going. The room we'd entered was blacker than the elevator and—wait. Three slivers of golden light trickled from the ceiling and onto the floor. I moved toward them, but couldn't make out any of the room's features. It was like stepping straight into midnight on an abandoned street.

A few seconds later, my eyes adjusted and I could finally see *something* beside black and three golden rays. The floors were concrete with jagged lumps scattered here and there. Rocks? My brow furrowed. Why were there rocks inside the room?

My palm brushed a wall, and I halted abruptly. I heard the others do the same.

"This is where you will learn to fight," a male voice said, only a short distance away. Ryan's voice. "Welcome."

I shivered.

He stepped into one of the muted beams, yet shadows still pulsed around him, hiding most of his face. He was a slash of dark in a room of black. "Jog in place while I speak," he said.

"Wh— what?" I asked, still reeling from his sudden presence.

"You heard me." His tone was stern, commanding. "Jog in place. All of you. Now."

Pushing out a breath, I hopped into motion. Elbows and knees slammed into me as the other girls did the same. Grunting, I spread out as best I could. Stupid darkness. (Stupid Ryan. He hadn't seemed overjoyed to hear my voice.)

"You'll fight most aliens at night," Ryan said, now amused. Could he see us? "So you must learn to fight them without seeing them. You'll fight most aliens outside, with nothing to cushion your falls. Therefore, you will train without any hint of softness underneath you."

All around me, I could hear the girls panting. My skin was already beading with sweat.

"You will be hurt during these training sessions," Ryan explained. "Get used to the idea now. I won't go easy on you, and I won't let you go easy on each other. The Outers won't."

He paused.

Please tell us we can stop jogging. Please tell us we can stop jogging. I'd gotten enough exercise with Mia.

He didn't, of course. "Starting out this way might seem cruel, but I'm actually doing you a favor. If you expect the worst, you'll be prepared for the worst. If you learn to fight past your exhaustion, you'll tap into a reservoir of strength you never knew you possessed."

Air burned in my lungs, but I didn't slow my gait.

Ryan spoke for another five minutes before ushering us to one of the side walls, which we had to feel our way to find. "Sit."

We did, finally able to catch our breath. Soon my eyes adjusted to the dark completely, and I was able to make Ryan out more clearly. And that, of course, was when he flipped on the lights. My lids blinked open and closed against the orange and red dots, trying to help my eyes adjust once again to the change.

When they did, I almost wished Ryan had left off the lights.

He looked good. Too good. Mouthwateringly good.

Today he was wearing a black T-shirt, black pants, and black boots. He was a shadow, even in the light. His dark hair was in disarray, and his blue eyes sparkled with amusement. To him, we probably looked like tired, sweaty lumps of shit.

"Are you ready to begin?" he asked. He met each and every girls' stare—except mine. Me, he avoided looking at altogether and that made me frown. That wasn't just a little rude of him, that was flat-out harsh.

What had I done? Had I made him mad?

I scoured my mind, replaying our last conversation, but couldn't think of anything I had done to offend him. With that realization came anger. He had no right to ignore me. He had no right to treat me as less than the others.

"Well," he commanded more coarsely. "Are. You. Ready?"

After everyone had nodded, he added more calmly, "Then let's do this."

For the next hour, he showed us a few hand moves and the best way to hit an Arcadian—chest and head, throat and temple. Groin. The lesson corresponded perfectly with our lesson from anatomy class, since we'd studied Arcadians there. They were vulnerable where humans were vulnerable, except their airways were located in different places.

As Ryan demonstrated the moves, there was a fluid grace to him that I'd never seen with another man. He almost looked like a dancer.

Finally he had us stand up and do the moves ourselves. The first was a punch forward with open palm to either break a nose or slam into the breastbone, cutting off the Arcadian's air supply.

Second, we learned a knee jerk and dive. We raised a knee, hard, then bent over, swooping our torsos in a wide half circle. The purpose, Ryan said, was to hurt our opponent, then avoid their strike of retaliation, which was sure to come.

"Mimic my actions," he said, kicking, straightening, turning, and kicking again. "Good, Kitten. Good, Jenn." He proceeded to congratulate everyone, his voice dripping with praise. Me, not so much. I got a "good," sure, but mine was muttered and he didn't say my name.

Maybe he *had* forgotten.

What the hell was going on with him?

Was everyone else the teacher's pet and I was just the unwanted slug? I ground my teeth together. I kicked straight, just as he'd done, then twirled and kicked again, his face a target in my mind. The girls, too, kicked and punched, then kicked again. I hadn't worked out in a long time (not counting Mia's workout and Ryan's jogging session) and after the first hour my muscles began burning. I began sweating—again.

Inside, I was cringing. Even though I was currently pissed off at Ryan, I didn't want him to see me like this. Truly, he'd only ever seen me at my worst. I mean, really. Not only was I sweating, but I was wearing the god-awful white pants and shirt every trainee was required to wear. And mine were a little too tight! Not good for a flat chest.

Kitten had taken—and needed—the larger clothing. Her breasts and hips were bigger than mine, a fact that would have made me jealous if Kitten weren't such a nice person.

"I need a volunteer," Ryan said, "to demonstrate the next move."

All the girls held up their hands. Except Emma, the tattooed one who hated all of us, and me, of course. Ryan still wouldn't look at me, and I wouldn't degrade myself by showing how eager I was to let him put his hands on me.

Deep down, though, I knew I'd like it—his hands on me, that is.

"Phoenix."

Hearing my name from him gave me an odd little shiver. I blinked in surprise. "Yeah?"

"Get up here." He waved me over, still looking anywhere but me.

"Lucky," Dani moaned.

My surprise intensifying, I walked slowly toward him. Each of my steps was measured, unsure. I couldn't help but wonder, *why me?* I mean, he *still* wouldn't glance in my direction. *Oh, wait,* I thought, frowning. He'd promised to be hard on us. He probably meant to pound me into the ground while "demonstrating."

No way. No damn way. I popped my jaw, an action born of irritation and one I'd done a lot more lately, and quickened my step. He wouldn't find amusement at my expense.

When I was within reaching distance, he clasped onto my shoulders and spun me around so that I faced the girls. Just as I'd known I would, I liked it. I liked his hands on me. They were big and warm and calloused, almost like a live wire. I could feel the heat of him seeping into me.

The girls' expressions ranged from envious to amused to wicked and back to envious. Ryan's body nearly touched mine, chest to back, but he maintained a safe distance away.

I'd been with guys, so intimacy was no stranger to me. But I'd been with them for all the wrong reasons. Curiosity. Lying to myself, thinking it was what I needed to do to feel good about who and what I was. Craving affection I couldn't seem to find anywhere else. Now, this time, I wanted a boy to hold me because of who *he* was.

Why couldn't I have been attracted to a student?

Ryan stepped closer, his body brushing mine. He was so close, I could feel his breath on the back of my neck, caressing. Goose bumps beaded over my skin. He squeezed my shoulders before wrapping his hands around my neck.

My eyes widened, and I gasped. The sensual haze that had trapped me finally dissipated. "What are you doing?"

He didn't release me, but squeezed harder. Not enough to cut off my air, but enough to consume my attention. "If an Arcadian grabs you from behind, how will you escape from him?"

Kitten raised her hand. "I know, I know!" Her golden cat's eyes practically glittered with eagerness.

Ryan motioned with his chin for her to continue, and his nose tickled the top of my head. I was battling a need to struggle, *not* to struggle, and to look cool and to prove myself. He wasn't hurting me, but he could at any moment.

"Kick backward and try to hit his balls."

Despite the situation, I pressed my lips together to keep

141

from laughing. The thought of kicking Ryan in the balls and dropping him to his knees was as appealing as it was appalling.

"That might work, as long as you do it calmly rather than in a panic and as long as he doesn't keep his body away from you, which is a possibility. Panic will fog your mind and quash your objective. You will miss your target every time and fail to realize key details, like the placement of the attacker's body." As he spoke, he traced his thumbs over my pulse points.

I shivered and tried to mask it with a cough. My cheeks flushed. No boy had ever touched me like this, as if I were a treasure of some sort. And that it was Ryan doing so . . . I licked my lips. Maybe I'd misread the situation. Maybe he wasn't mad at me, after all.

"Your new motto is: Whatever means necessary," he said. "Say it with me: Whatever means necessary."

We did.

"Good. Again."

We repeated it a second time.

"There are several things you can do," he added. "First, however, you should scream—if possible—so that he'll hopefully remove one of his hands from your neck to cover your mouth. Also, screaming might bring you aid and alert your teammates to your whereabouts."

Good idea. I opened my mouth to scream, but Ryan laughed. "Not yet," he said.

I pressed my lips together.

"Won't screaming draw civilians and perhaps get them killed?" Cara asked.

"If it's your only resort, it's a chance you'll have to take," Ryan replied. "The good news is, a civilian could also work as a distraction, giving you the opportunity you need to free yourself and kill the alien, which is your ultimate objective."

"But, what if screaming doesn't work?" Johanna asked.

Cara nodded. "Yeah, I mean, some Outers won't care if you draw attention. They might even like it."

"If he doesn't release you with one hand to cover your mouth, elbow him in the breastbone with all of your strength. Remember, that's where an Arcadian's main airway is located."

"And if *that* doesn't work?" Kitten said.

"Stomp his instep and stomp hard. Stomp repeatedly if you must, but stomp fast. Pinch his thigh, drawl blood. Tug on his hair. Time is your enemy in this position and you must get him to loosen his hold as soon as possible. Hurt him and he'll let go, giving you the opportunity to turn and punch."

The girls nodded, awed, rapt.

Ryan didn't remove his hands from my neck, but increased the pressure. "Now," he said.

"What?" I gasped out. He still wasn't hurting me, but the extra force was frightening.

"Break free," he commanded me.

I tried to laugh, but couldn't quite manage it. The girls

watched us with worried expressions. "You want me to fight you?"

"Break free," he said again, this time with more force. He squeezed harder, and this time it *hurt.* "I heard you passed your drug test," he whispered, his breath caressing my ear. "Congrats."

Thanks for the reminder that I'm the drug addict here. "I won't get in trouble for hurting you?" I wheezed, having trouble drawing in a breath.

"You can't hurt me. Now fight, damn it, before you pass out."

I wasn't going to pass out. No way. After I'd helped Ryan fight the Sybilins, he—more than anyone—should have had more faith in my abilities. "I'm not sure I can," I managed to gasp out, playing the nervous little girl. "You're hurting me."

His hold loosened. "You can, Phoenix. You just need—"

While he spoke, I acted. And I acted hard, just like he'd said. *Whatever means necessary.* I didn't hold back. Draw blood? My pleasure. I propelled my elbow into his stomach. Air whooshed from him, and he doubled over. His hands loosened even more.

I'd probably just aced the test with that move, but I pinched his thigh, anyway. As he howled, I slammed my foot into his instep.

Pivoting on my heel, I turned around and slugged him in the nose. His head whipped to the side. My knuckles throbbed, still bruised from the pounding I'd given the Sybilins.

I stood there, panting and facing my instructor, triumph washing through me. A trickle of blood dripped from his nose. Test complete. I'd escaped.

Slowly Ryan righted himself and faced me. His blue eyes were practically glowing as he wiped away the blood with the back of his hand. His lips twitched.

"I broke free," I said, chin raised, "by whatever means necessary."

"So you did," he returned, and there was a pleased edge to the words.

Behind us, Kitten clapped and whooped. "That's my girl!"

Ryan smiled fully. "If I was giving a grade today, you'd get an A for kicking my ass."

"Lucky," Dani said again.

"Thank you," I said, proud of myself. The throb in my hand increased with every second that passed, but it was worth it.

Suddenly Ryan's eyes narrowed. Something dark flashed inside them, something dangerous. I blinked, certain I was mistaken. I hadn't done or said anything to warrant that kind of reaction.

"You did that a little too well," he said. "Anyone ever tried to choke you before?"

Worried? About me? How sweet! Exasperation drained from me, and pleasure took its place. "No. That was a first." And an experience I'd rather not repeat.

Bit by bit, his expression softened. "Well, you did great."

I smiled over at him. His gaze dropped to my mouth. Heat infused his expression this time, and he took a step toward me. Did he . . . did he want to kiss me? The very thought excited me. His lips on mine . . . his taste in my mouth. . . . He seemed to catch himself, though, and froze for a split second. He inched backward.

"Get back in line," he commanded stiffly.

He was changing moods faster than I could keep up. What had brought on the sudden change *this* time? "Ryan," I said.

"In line, Germaine," he snapped.

Unmoving, I frowned at him.

"Line. Now."

Shaking my head at his behavior, I spun around and claimed my place at the wall. Cara was peering over at me, her expression weird.

What? I mouthed. I didn't need crap from her, too.

Nothing, she mouthed back and turned away.

I nudged her with my shoulder. *What?*

Her dark brows arched, and I could tell she was trying to hold back a grin. *I thought he was just okay.*

My eyes slitted. *Whatever.*

Ryan cleared his throat, then launched into a lecture about everything I'd done right and a few things I could have done better. Like hitting his throat or his temple for maximum damage instead of hitting his nose.

After that, he explained what we would be learning in his

class for the rest of the year, fighting skills that would correlate with our alien anatomy class. "In the end, you'll be able to fight anyone and anything. You'll be able to kill with your bare hands."

Kitten's stomach rumbled, and all eyes turned to her. Her cheeks flushed a rosy red, and she began licking her arm and rubbing it over her chin. A nervous habit, I guess.

"Hungry?" Ryan asked her with a grin.

She nodded reluctantly.

"Good, because it's chow time. Go on. Get out of here. You girls did very well today."

We didn't need to be told twice. We pounded from the cage. But I couldn't help myself. I tossed a glance over my shoulder. Ryan was watching me, and that strange heat was back in his eyes . . .

———

Breakfast was served in a cafeteria very similar to the one at my school, just smaller. The food, though, was much better. Thank God! Fresh fruit and warm nuts, baked breads, syn-chicken, and rice. It was like dining in a five-star restaurant. The only difference was, we didn't get to choose what we wanted.

We placed our hands on the ID box at the counter, endured a quick scan, and then a tray made specifically for us was slid down a tube and into our direction. The entire process took less than a minute. Very cool, yet very military.

"They like to keep us healthy and proteined up," Cara said, sitting beside me at the table.

The rest of the class joined us after they'd gotten their trays. We weren't the only ones in the cafeteria. Only girls were present, though. Of the few that were there with us, some cast us curious glances. Some turned their noses up at us. One even "accidentally" bumped into us, telling us to "stay out of the way, weaklings."

There was a lot of confidence in the room, a lot of cockiness. "What did you guys do to get sent here? And," I added after swallowing a bite of rice, "how long have you been here?"

"Got arrested for assault," Dani said with a shrug. "And I've been here two fun-filled days."

So I wasn't the only criminal. I shouldn't have taken comfort in that, but I did.

"Kadar found me living—" Lindsay pressed her lips together, as if she didn't want to reveal the information. She waved her hand through the air and strove for a casual tone. "He saved me from an Outer. I've been here two days, as well."

"My mom knows Boss and called and begged him to take me," Jenn said. There was a trace of bitterness in her tone. "She didn't have what it took to work in this field, so she's leaving it up to me to live her dream." She forced a laugh. "I've been here several weeks, but this is my first class."

"What about you?" Cara asked me, her dark eyes curious. "What'd you do?"

I told them about the night the Sybilins attacked. They became very quiet, and studied me more intently. By the time I finished, they were staring at me with awe. And perhaps disbelief.

Dani blinked over at me. "A Sybilin. S-Y-B-I-L-I-N. I knew you'd fought with Ryan Stone, but I'd assumed— I don't know what I'd assumed. Just not a Sybilin."

I nodded, brow puckered. "Well, it's true."

"But . . . the Sybilins are a myth. Aren't they?" Lindsay's red eyebrows arched as she searched the other faces.

"I promise you they're very real." We ate in silence for a few minutes. A few more girls walked past our table, muttering, "Weaklings." "What's that about?" I asked.

Jenn tugged at the ends of her hair, the black curls bouncing back into place. "The facility begins new classes every three months. You'll notice that each new class has less and less girls. Some have been here only three months, others six, others nine. The ones who have survived it all and have been here twelve months think of everyone else as know-nothing weaklings."

"Their classes are in different hallways," Cara added after she swallowed a bit of banana, "so the only time we have to deal with them is at lunch and social hour."

"Are there ever any fights?" Kitten asked, her eagerness clear.

"I've heard of a few." Jenn leaned into us, her voice dropping. "One even ended in death. The girl responsible was memory-wiped and returned home. Or so I heard." Straightening, she nibbled on the edge of her syn-chicken and closed her eyes in surrender. "God, this is good. I thought I'd die after all that exercise."

"Where are the boys?" Kitten glanced around. I think she wanted to know where Bradley was and what he looked like. Not that she'd mentioned him recently, but I still suspected she considered him off limits to everyone else. "Jenn?"

"What, am I an instructor?" Jenn splayed her arms wide. "I don't know all the answers."

"You sure?" I said with a laugh. I drained my milk. I would have preferred soda, but whatever. "You know a lot more than us."

"Fine. I know the answer to this one, too." Jenn pinched a piece of bread and shrugged. "The boys are in a separate building, but we'll get to see them three times a week. The powers that be let us get together so we won't try and sneak over there."

"How do you know so much?" Kitten asked, incredulous. She licked the edge of her milk carton.

"I told you. My mom and Boss are friends. When I was recruited, he had a long talk with me about what to expect."

"What I wouldn't do to trade places with you," Kitten said and threw a roll at her. "After my interview, I got a tour of a restricted hallway and locked in my room with Phoenix."

Jenn caught the bread, chuckled, and took an exaggerated bite before tossing it back. I leaned back in my chair, realizing I was happier in that moment than I'd been in a long time. These girls were nice, and I enjoyed their company.

To them, I was just one of the girls.

It was sad to think that some of us would soon be kicked out. And it was embarrassing to think that I'd probably be the first. I'd be smart to keep everyone here at a distance.

But when have I ever been smart?

10

My third class of the day turned out to be Weapons 101.

Kadar was the instructor, and he definitely knew what he was talking about. I'd never seen anyone more at ease with guns and knives. It was scary. He made Ryan and Allison look like amateurs as he held up each weapon, told us about it (and what we'd be expected to do with it), then demonstrated its use.

Finally he said, "Line up. You've each been assigned a stall."

We rushed to obey. I found my stall at the very end, close to the wall. This classroom was different from any of the others. We were inside a large arena with multiple booths, or "stalls," as Kadar had called them. Each stall offered a waist-high counter and a long, narrow pathway with a target perched at the end. (Each target was a different type of Outer.)

My target just happened to be a Sybilin.

"Thought you'd appreciate that," Kadar told me with a grin.

"I do."

"Prove it by nailing him during practice."

"I'll do my best," I said, and I meant it. I'd never fired a gun before, but I was suddenly determined to impress Kadar with my "skill."

"Good. All right, everyone," he said, moving away from me to pace in front of the group. "You'll switch stalls every day. Don't want you to get complacent. Now," he continued, "on your counter, you'll find a pyre-gun, a throwing star, and a heat-seeking minigrenade. I know I showed you how to use them, but do any of you have an idea just how much damage those items can do?"

"They kill," Kitten said, rubbing her hands together in anticipation. "That's all we need to know."

Frowning, Kadar shook his head. "They can kill your opponent, yes. But they can also kill or maim *you*. That is what you need to know."

Jenn looked from the weapons to Kadar, from Kadar to the weapons. She paled. "You said 'maim'. What kind of damage are we talking about here?"

He withdrew a pyre-gun from his waist and held it out for our inspection. "This has three settings. Hot. Hotter. And flames of hell. You can dial each setting like this." He pinched his fingers on a small black dial and twisted toward the right.

I heard several oohs and ahs.

"Hot will fry your target to a crisp, but they'll probably live to tell the tale. Hotter will kill everything it touches: skin, bone, organ. There's still a chance the target can survive, depending on where you shoot him. Flames of hell will kill your target and anyone standing next to it."

There were a few more oohs and ahs.

I glanced down at my pyre-gun, drinking in every detail. "There are no numbers on the dial," I pointed out. "How will we know that we've programmed the right setting?"

"You'll learn the difference." In the blink of an eye, Kadar spun around and fired at the wall beside us.

I yelped as an amber beam erupted, splitting the room into white and yellow. Spots blinked in front of my eyes. Even where I stood, at the end of the procession line, I felt the heat of the beam, and air burned in my throat.

Eyes wide, I glanced at the wall and saw a black, sizzling circle. I gulped.

What if someone shot me with one of those?

Okay. Back to being unsure about the decision to stay here.

"That wall is comprised of a special metal that will not melt under the hottest of flames, and yet it was blackened. Imagine what the beam could do to something that *will* melt." He paused, each second causing the room to thicken with tension. "If you accidentally shoot yourself with this . . ." Kadar didn't finish his sentence. He let us finish it in our minds. We'd die. No doubt about it.

"Uh, I'm not sure I want to carry one of those," Jenn said, her voice shaking.

Cara shook her head, dark hair swishing at her temples. "Me, either."

Kadar rolled his eyes. "Has anyone ever fired a gun before? Not just a pyre-gun, but any type of gun?"

I shook my head, a perfect imitation of Cara. Only Emma raised her hand, and the action was tentative, as if she feared getting in trouble.

"What kind of gun?" Kadar asked her. I was surprised by the gentleness of his tone.

Emma's gaze swept over us nervously, and I noticed she was twisting the sides of her pants with her hands. Her skin was so pale, her tattoo stood out more than usual. "An antique. With bullets."

He nodded. "Good, sweetheart. That's good. How was your aim?"

Sweetheart? She shrugged and gazed down at her boots. "Okay, I guess."

"Did you hit what you were aiming at?"

"No," she admitted softly.

"Well, you will soon." He stopped in the middle of us and locked his hands behind his back. In that moment, he looked like the quintessential army commander. "I've removed the detonation crystal from each of your guns, so you don't have to worry about frying yourselves or each other—today. That'll come later. All your gun will emit is a harmless beam of light."

Relief swam through me, as did anticipation. I'd never even held a gun before. My mom found them too dangerous to keep in the house.

"Pick them up," Kadar said, watching us intently.

I turned to face my counter. The gun was still there, in the middle, staring up at me. It had a black handle, an iridescent center that was clear and bumpy. The barrel was long, thin, and silver. Even though I knew it couldn't fire, my hand shook as I reached out and wrapped my fingers around it and hefted it up.

My brow wrinkled. The gun was lighter than it appeared, weighing no more than a syn-apple.

"Learn it," Kadar said. "If you treat it right, that little baby will save your life over and over again."

Little baby. A cute name for a deadly piece of machinery. Somehow, though, it fit. I closed my eyes and allowed my hands to "learn" the weapon, to gauge its nuances. Would my mom freak if she found out what I was doing right now or would she be proud for what I was going to do to protect her? Either way. . . .

"Like it?"

Kadar's question reverberated in my mind as I caressed my thumb over the barrel. "Oh yeah," I said. I opened my eyes and grinned.

No one else responded. Were the other girls not as entranced with their weapons as I was? I peeked over at them, lined up beside me as they were. Some were already aiming, some were studying the intricacies of the inside chamber.

My grin spread. They liked, too. They liked a lot. There was something so powerful about holding a weapon like this. Something so safe. No one could hurt me. I was invincible.

"Aim," Kadar said.

I did without hesitation. I closed one eye and extended my arms, the fake Sybilin in sight. I pointed the barrel straight ahead, holding steady. Would I be able to hit my target on the first try? Only one way to find out.

"Squeeze the trigger."

My finger curled around it, and I squeezed. I expected a *click,* a ray of light, but heard nothing. No sound. No light, either. What I didn't expect was something solid to actually fly out of the barrel, but it did. I gasped, and I heard several other girls do the same.

Had I hit my target? My gaze narrowed on the fake Sybilin, searching . . . searching . . . I grinned when I spotted a red protrusion on its right shoulder. I'd been aiming for its heart, but, hey, I'd managed to hit it on the first try!

Go me!

"I think my gun is broken. It didn't make a sound," Jenn said, twisting the weapon in every direction. Even her own. "And there was no light."

Kadar leapt toward her and whisked the gun from her grip. "Watch where you point this. You could have shot your own face. I lied about the light to relax you. Today we're using darts, but even those can hurt you."

She paled. "Sorry. My bad."

"The pyre-gun was designed for silence." He handed it back to her, the barrel facing the floor. "Sometimes you have to dial and fire with an enemy nearby and you don't want that enemy to know your location."

Ah. That made total sense.

"Your pyre-gun also has a stun setting. All you have to do is twist the dial to the left until it can't twist anymore. But stun only works on other-worlders. Repeat after me: Stun will not work on humans."

Silence. What was with all the repeating? We weren't children.

He frowned. "Have I been too nice? Do you think it's okay to ignore my orders? Repeat what I said!"

"Stun will not work on humans," we said in unison.

"Only aliens," he said.

"Only aliens," we repeated.

Kadar nodded with satisfaction. "Something about the alignment of human skin cells causes the stun to bounce off rather than absorb. We're currently testing a device that will work on humans. Sometimes they're worse than the other-worlders you're chasing." His disgust rang out loud and clear. "Sympathizers will try and hurt *you*, rather than allow you to hurt an alien, no matter its crimes."

"They suck," Cara muttered.

"Maybe we need a how-to-take-down-a-sympathizer class," Dani suggested.

Kadar continued as if they hadn't spoken. "The fire settings, however, will work on both humans and aliens. Make sure you want to injure or kill your target before you fire."

Jenn raised her hand. Her brown eyes were wide, and she looked upset. "But . . . what if we don't want to stun or kill?"

He answered her question with a question of his own. "Your targets will be predatory aliens and the humans who help them. Why would you *not* want to stun or kill them?"

She nibbled on her bottom lip. Poor thing. It was so obvious she didn't want to be here, didn't want to learn how to fight. Or kill. She was being forced to learn by her mom, by the superfreaky Boss and what *they* wanted for her life.

At least they cared about her, you know? They wanted the best for her. *No jealousy, missy.*

"Let's get back to work," Kadar said. "Hold the gun at your side." There were two heartbeats of silence as he waited for us to comply. "Good. Now aim and fire, as quickly as possible."

We did. I missed the target this time. So did a lot of the girls, judging by the numerous moans I heard. I'd been tense, determined, rather than relaxed like before. Crap.

"Again," Kadar said.

Quickly I aimed and fired. Missed. The dart sailed over my target's wrinkled shoulder.

"Again."

Relax. Just relax. Once again, I aimed and fired. This time, I nailed the Sybilin in the stomach. I'd aimed at its heart, so hitting his stomach wasn't optimal. It was a success, though, and I grinned.

Kadar leveled a pointed stare at me. "Keep firing until you're consistently hitting what you aim at or until your gun runs out of darts. And by the way, there are one hundred of the little suckers in the clip."

"No way," Jenn said, holding her gun up for inspection.

"One hundred," Lindsay moaned. She hooked several strands of red hair behind her ears. "So far I haven't hit anything."

"For real?" Dani said, incredulous. "We have to keep at this until we run out?"

I peered at the gun. "You're kidding, right? Nothing this small can hold so many darts."

"Uh, yes it can. The darts expand upon release," he explained. "Did any of you read your manual? You're supposed to forget everything you think you know. Open your minds. Nothing is impossible here."

"Except stunning humans with a pyre-gun," I muttered.

"I heard that," Kadar said, but he didn't sound angry. He sounded amused. "Now get to work."

Over and over I repeated the process, not stopping until I was able to aim and fire in one fluid motion—and actually achieve success more often than not. Unfortunately, I wasn't the first (and my competitive spirit didn't like that fact). Johanna was, followed by Dani, then me.

"All right." Kadar clapped his hands. "Our time is up for today."

Emma was the only one who hadn't hit the target. I

glanced over and studied what she'd been aiming at. It was a bright blue creature I didn't recognize, with shiny skin, a lithe body, and webbed hands and feet. Her darts were spread all around it. Her expression was blank as she lowered her gun onto the counter, and her hand was shaking. There were lines of tension bracketing her eyes.

"I'm so proud of you girls I'm going to do you a favor." Kadar leaned against the wall and crossed his arms over his chest. "Tomorrow I'm going to let you fire your guns with the detonation crystals inside rather than the dart clips."

The moisture in my mouth dried as excitement and apprehension fought for dominance inside me. "Are you sure we're ready?"

"No," he said with a grin. "That's the beauty of it."

One wrong move, and I could fry any one of my new friends. One wrong move, and any one of my new friends could fry *me*. I'd probably have nightmares. And yet, it gave me an even greater sense of power than before, the thought of firing an actual weapon. Of being tough and lethal. Of facing down my enemy—fake target though it was.

"You're free to rest in your rooms or relax in the Common," Kadar said then. "Your next class isn't for another hour."

Remaining in line, we filed from the room. Or rather, I tried to. Kadar grabbed my arm and pulled me aside. I blinked up at him in confusion and dread. He wore a serious expression, his eyes dark, his beard stubble more prominent. "Something wrong?" I asked.

"I'm sorry, but you can't go with the others. You have an appointment with Angel. She's a . . . doctor."

"What? Why? I'm not sick."

He didn't explain. "She's in room eight, and she's waiting." He gave me a gentle push toward the door. "She doesn't like to be kept waiting."

Freaking great. Another drug test, most likely. I hated that I was being put through that when I hadn't done anything wrong. I hadn't done anything to cause these A.I.R. agents to lose faith in me.

"I'm not going to stand for this," I told Kaden through gritted teeth.

His mouth twitched, but he didn't smile. "Just go to room eight, little girl."

<hr />

"So . . . how are your new classes?"

"Good." I shifted on the plush red couch, a glass of water in hand. Angel was not a medical doctor as I'd assumed, and she hadn't given me a drug test. No, she was some sort of psychiatrist. And she wanted to probe my mind. *How do you feel? Are you sad? Blah, blah, blah.*

I'd been to what felt like hundreds of this type of session, where a kind, gentle, *understanding* soul tried to learn all my secrets, all the reasons I did the things that I did.

I could save them the trouble: it had seemed fun at the

time. There was nothing more to it than that. Okay, maybe I'd been pissed at my dad. Maybe I'd wanted to lash out at him. Maybe I'd wanted to forget and feel something besides pain. That didn't mean I needed therapy.

"Having any trouble?" she asked.

"Nope." God, when would this end?

"I'm glad," she said.

"Yep. Me, too."

She was a very attractive woman, though she lacked the stunning beauty of the other ladies I'd seen here. She had light brown hair that was pulled back in a twist, brown eyes, and lots of freckles. Very unassuming. Very unthreatening. And yet . . .

There was something about her. I couldn't look away. Didn't want to look away. She radiated a trust-me vibe, a gentleness that was very soothing.

"Do we really have to do this?" I asked with a weary sigh. "I'm doing good, I feel good, and I haven't done anything wrong. I even passed the drug test."

She *tsk*ed under her tongue. "Regardless of how good you feel, regardless of what you've done and what you haven't done, regardless of what you've passed, we really have to do this. So drink your water, please, and relax."

"I'm not thirsty."

"You just left a very grueling combat class, followed by an intense weapons class. I don't want you becoming dehydrated."

"Fine." I drained the glass and held it out for her inspection. "No more dehydration worries."

One corner of her mouth curled. "Should I give you a gold star?" She didn't wait for my response, but claimed the glass and set it beside a cup of blue-tinted liquid resting on a nearby table.

"Why do I need a therapy session, anyway?" I grumbled. "None of the other girls have to do it." *That I knew of,* I silently amended.

"All the girls will speak with me at one time or another."

"I'm lucky first, though, right?"

She didn't try to deny it. "None of the other girls are former Onadyn users," she stated bluntly.

Mia was fond of reminding me; Ryan was found of reminding me. It wasn't like I'd forget. My eyes narrowed on her. "The key word is 'former.' I no longer use."

She shrugged, unimpressed with my fervency. "A user is a user, dear. There is no such thing as 'former.'"

I gritted my molars.

"To be honest," she said, uncrossing and recrossing her legs, "I'm surprised you were even allowed into the program."

Not that again. None of them were really giving me a chance. "I deserve to be here." The complete opposite of what I'd first thought about the camp. But as I spoke, a wave of *something* swept through my brain. Something odd. A fog, maybe. A sense of acceptance. My shoulders relaxed into the couch, and all of my muscles seemed to melt into the soft fabric. My blood warmed and my heartbeat quickened. "I'm having . . . there's something wrong with me."

"No. You're fine." Her face swam in and out of my vision. "Breathe deeply," she said. "That's it. In. Out. You're simply tired from physical exertion."

With every breath, my strength *did* return. My eyesight cleared, and my heartbeat slowed.

"Good?"

I nodded.

"As to your deservedness, we'll see." Her stare was intent, probing. "This is a tough place to live and sometimes severe stress can send an addict back to their habit."

True. It had happened to me once before, the first time I left rehab. Only two weeks had passed before I'd started using again. The temptation had been too great. I'd fallen when I'd overheard my mom talking on the phone to my dad. She'd called and asked him to take me for a drive, to a movie, something, anything to get to know me again, telling him I needed a male influence in my life. He'd refused.

I'd cried and cried and cried, and then I'd gotten high. The downward spiral had once again begun. Drugs, boys. A total lack of concern for the people around me.

My hands clenched into tight fists. "I'm not going to fly," I told Angel. "I'm not going to drink Breathless. I'm not going to puff it or inject it. I don't like the girl I become when I do."

Angel's chin canted to the side. "What kind of girl is that?"

My cheeks heated, but I didn't soften the truth. "A liar. A thief. A . . . slut. Violent. Untrustworthy."

"And what kind of girl do you want to be?"

Uh, duh. "The complete opposite. Honorable. Trust-worthy."

"I'm glad to hear you say that." She tapped her bloodred nails on her bare knee. Her skirt had ridden up, revealing several inches of her thigh. "I'd really like to continue our conversation about your classes. You never answered me. What do you like about them?"

I propped my elbows on my knees and dropped my head into my hands. *Just tell her the truth and get it over with. I want to be trustworthy, remember.* "I like most of it. The instructors need to do a better job of treating us like adults and some of the stupid rules need to be rescinded."

"Which rules?"

"All of them," I said, not wanting to single out the dating rule.

She rolled her eyes. "Tell me about your classmates. Do you like them?"

"Yes."

"Even Emma? I hear she hasn't spoken a word to you."

"She's not bad," I answered truthfully. I didn't know what else to say. I didn't dislike Emma. There was something about her that struck a cord inside me. Sympathy, maybe? I knew what it was like to be the girl everyone hated.

Angel shifted in her seat. "I heard you fought a group of

Sybilins a few days before you arrived at camp. Is that true?"

"Apparently you hear a lot of things," I muttered. She made me feel like I'd been spied on. *Hello. I probably had been.* "If you don't mind, I'd rather not talk about that night."

"Phoenix."

That was it; that was all she said. But I found myself sitting up, shoulders squared, spine straight. "Yes?"

"You want to answer my question."

Yes, I thought, a little dazed, I wanted to answer her question. "I did fight a group of Sybilins," I found myself saying. I frowned.

"Did you feel guilty afterward?"

I shook my head, bringing myself out of that strange bemusement. "For?" I relaxed against the couch. Thank God she hadn't asked about Ryan. If I admitted to being attracted to him, would I be ordered to stay away from him?

"Did you feel guilty for hurting another living thing?"

"No. I didn't." Truth.

"Why is that, do you think?"

"I had to stop them. They were evil and would have killed my friends."

Again, she arched a brow. "And not you?"

"No."

"Interesting." She lifted a digital notebook from the table and balanced it on her lap. Typing, she muttered, "That's very interesting."

"Not really," I said.

Pausing, she glanced up. "And why is that?"

"I wouldn't have let them."

Slowly her lips stretched into a smile. That smile lit up her entire face and made her . . . beautiful. Somehow more beautiful than even the perfect Le'Ace. Her skin glowed, her eyes became alive. Liquid amber. This woman was mesmerizing. "Good answer."

"Honest answer."

She typed something else in the notebook. "Let's talk about your mother's rejection of you the morning after the fight."

The bottom dropped out of my stomach. No way. I was *not* going there. "She didn't reject me," I managed to say. Lie. She had. She'd practically pushed me out the door and hadn't cared enough to say good-bye. That knowledge still cut deeply. *She'll love me again. Once I've made something of myself.*

Angel frowned over at me. "Yes, she did and you know it. She kicked you out of her house and out of her life."

"So?" I jolted upright, pinning the doctor with a fierce stare. A wave of dizziness hit me, and I rubbed my temples. "What do you want from me? What do you want me to say? Yes, she rejected me. Yes, she kicked me out. Happy?"

She gave no outward reaction to my fury. "Why the hostility? I merely asked you a question."

"And I asked you a question. What exactly do you want from me?"

She crossed her arms over her chest, showing no mercy. "I

want to hear about your mother and how you felt when she called the camp."

Fine. She wanted to hear, she'd hear. "Like shit, okay? I felt like shit. She knew how my father's abandonment hurt me, and yet she treated me the same way." The words poured from me, and I didn't even try to stop them. "I'm her daughter, but she couldn't wait to get rid of me." Tears filled my eyes, burning. I angrily swiped them away. "Happy now?"

"Yes," she said, surprising me. "Anger is good, Phoenix. Anger is very good."

"Why? Aren't we supposed to let go of our anger?"

"Only after you've dealt with it. Besides, if you'd felt nothing, that would have meant you were suppressing your emotions. If you were suppressing your emotions, you would one day have a breakdown. And when an agent has a breakdown, bad things happen, to the agent and to everyone around her." Angel dug in the pocket of her suit jacket and slapped something on the coffee table between us.

I glanced down, and my jaw fell open. Need and fear raced through me. A tremor traveled the length of my spine. "Why are you doing this to me?"

"How do you feel, looking at that?" she asked, remaining in her seat.

I tried to look at her, but I could not tear my gaze from the vial of Onadyn lying so innocently in front of me. It was small and clear. Beguiling. My mouth watered. "I feel . . . thirsty," I said honestly, hoarsely.

"And?"

"And I hate myself for that thirst." The words tore from me.

"Why?"

"I told you. I know what happens when I use. My brain begins to malfunction and I can't think clearly. I do such stupid, horrible things." God, did I do stupid things. Sadly, that day on the school steps wasn't an isolated incident. I'd degraded my mother in front of so many people, time and time again.

More than that, I'd once woken up in bed with a boy I hadn't known. Hadn't wanted to know, really. And I hadn't been able to remember what we'd done. I'd once stolen a bottle of scented enzyme mist from a store and was arrested within minutes.

The list could go on and on.

"Take it away," I said weakly. "Please."

"No. I want you to pick it up."

"No." Violently I shook my head. Tendrils of hair slapped at my cheeks, but didn't tear me from the Onadyn's spell.

"Pick it up," she commanded. It was the first time she'd used such a stern, unbending tone of voice with me.

"No!"

"Pick it up, Phoenix, or I'll recommend that you're kicked out of the camp."

The one thing that could make me obey. I liked this camp. I didn't want to leave yet. Still I hesitated.

"Pick. It. Up."

"I hate you," I hissed, finally reaching out. My fingers

closed around the vial. "What kind of mind doctor are you, torturing me like this?"

She ignored my question. "Smell it."

My hands didn't hesitate to obey. Without thought, I brought the vial to my nose and sniffed, savoring the scent of dew-kissed rain. Hmmm, so good. So delicious.

Poison, my mind said.

Sweet, my body replied. *One taste. One little sip.* What could it hurt?

In the end, I tossed it at Angel. The plastic vial nailed her in the shoulder. "*You* hold it," I snarled at her.

For a long while, she didn't move or comment. Finally, she pinched the vial between her fingers and stuffed it back into her pocket. She gave me another of those enthralling smiles. "Under stress, and still you turned it away."

I raised my chin. "That's right."

"Good."

"Bitch," I growled.

She didn't lose her smile. "I want you to know, Phoenix, that it's not because your mother stopped loving you that she pushed you away. It's *because* she loves you that she did it."

The switch of topics was jarring, but I welcomed it. The Onadyn was gone, out of my sight, out of reaching distance. I could handle anything else that was thrown at me. "I don't understand."

"I met with her this morning, just so you know. She's terrified of watching you waste away, of watching you die, and telling you good-bye was more than she could have endured. Not after she watched your father walk away."

The mention of my dad caused my stomach to twist painfully.

"Your mother wants you to have the life she herself could not," Angel said.

"How can you be sure?" I asked past the sudden lump in my throat. In my mind, I replayed the last few minutes I'd had with my mom, studying her face, her eyes. They *were* tortured, I realized. Her body had been stiff, as if preparing for a blow. Her eyes had been watery, as if she'd been holding back tears. I gulped. Almost sobbed.

"You have a core of iron inside you," Angel said, "a core that scares and intimidates those who do not possess the same. They know they cannot control you and flounder with how to deal with you."

I didn't respond. I couldn't. A multitude of emotions swirled through me: shock, doubt, hope, joy, relief, and anger.

"Think about what I said, all right?"

Slowly I nodded.

"Good." Angel waved to the door. "Get out of here. You have things to do, and this session is over."

I didn't move. "Do I—get to stay at camp, then?"

"For now," she said, as if it had never been in question. "Just know that you, more than anyone, can never let your guard down. You have to stay two steps ahead of the game or you will always be seen as second best."

Frowning, I stood and moved toward the door. Her next words stopped me, however. "Just so you know, there was a truth serum in the water you drank. The fact that you were still able to resist the drug is astonishing and something to be proud of."

What? I spun around. "Truth serum?"

"Here, drink this." She lifted the cup of blue-tinted liquid beside her, stood, and closed the distance between us. "It will combat the effects of what I gave you, so you don't reveal any secrets to your new friends."

She could be lying, but I didn't care. I didn't want to take the risk. I drained the contents. Grinning, she wrapped her arms around me and gave me a hug.

I hadn't been hugged in so many years I almost didn't know what to do. Almost. Tentatively, my arms wound around her, too. I wasn't sure if I liked her, but I couldn't have stopped myself from hugging her if a pyre-gun had been aimed at my head.

"Anytime you want to talk," she said, "I'm here."

11
———

The next day, after all our classes—and another therapy session for me (sigh)—it was party time. Or rather, time to "get to know each other." We weren't to be given any beer, of course, but we had been told we'd get to listen to music, play games (video, virtual, and pool), and eat tons of food. Good-for-us food, but that was better than nothing.

"Get to know each other," Mia repeated when we reached the threshold of a crowded but spacious room. Already I could hear the *bump, bump,* and grind of rock. "Get to know the older girls and get to know the boys. But don't forget, even for a second, that we'll be watching you. You know the rules." Having said her piece, she was off, leaving us in an open doorway.

My shock that we'd get to spend time with the male trainees—and instructors?—barely had time to register before the girls surged forward. One of them grabbed hold of my arm and tugged me inside. All too soon I was standing on the fringes of the party. The room was dimly lit, filled to capacity, and cracking with laughter and conversation.

I experienced a shiver of nervousness.

Everyone around me seemed to know where to stand, how to stand, and what to do. I couldn't force my brain to work right. Should I smile? Or would that make me look too easy? Should I wave or was that something only losers did?

Should I dance or was that something only the older girls were allowed to do? Speaking of the older, more experienced girls, none of them cared to help us or welcome us.

There was a definite hierarchy here. A tier of importance—at least in the older girls' minds. Obviously they thought they were better than us. Fine. Whatever. Maybe one day, we'd feel the same about new recruits. Until then, I considered it a stupid mind-set.

Everything's going to be fine. I released a long, drawn-out sigh, taking in the sea of white clothing I saw. The only difference between the kids—fashion-wise—was skin and hair color. I'd fit right in, so that was one worry I could cross out.

Why are you still standing here? Do something!

"Ohmygod, I'm on sensory overload," Jenn said.

"Want to, I don't know, mingle?" I asked the girls.

"Not yet. I'm scoping," Cara said, sounding as nervous as I felt.

They might look in control, but they didn't feel it and that comforted me. I wasn't the only one.

"This place is delectable," Kitten said, sounding as eager for action as ever.

Okay, she was the exception.

The floor was black and white tile, almost dizzying. A strobe hung from the ceiling. Holographs of movie stars danced in each of the corners. Several tables were piled high with the promised food, and there were couches and plush syn-fur chairs to relax upon.

From the corner of my eye, I saw Emma stride to a far, empty corner and disappear in the shadows. I frowned. "What's Emma's problem?"

Dani waved a hand through the air, wisping strands of light hair in front of her eyes. She brushed them aside. "Who knows?"

"I do," Jenn answered. Dark eyes glistening, she leaned toward us and whispered, "Don't tell anyone, okay, because I totally don't want to become the gossip, but she was out swimming one day and was raped by a group of Lyrosses."

Shock coursed through me, followed quickly by sympathy. I'd never heard of a Lyross, but rape was rape.

Jenn must have sensed my puzzlement because she added, "Not a lot is known about them, but we have learned that they came through the portals a few years ago and now live in our oceans."

Okay. I was sooo never going swimming again. Why the hell was information like that kept quiet? That was something people had a right to know. I wondered how many other human women had been raped by them while swimming.

Lindsay's face softened. "Poor thing. Raped." She shuddered.

"That's awful." Features sad, Johanna placed a hand over her heart. "Just . . . awful. My sister was raped by a boyfriend, and I remember the hell she went through during recovery."

"How do you know all of this?" I asked Jenn.

"Duh. I know just about everything because Boss tells my mom. I think they're—" She stopped, her mocha-colored features contorting as she made a gagging sound "—lovers. Anyway, Emma tried to kill herself afterward and was brought here when she recovered. They want to channel her rage, make her a cold assassin, like Le'Ace, or an unstoppable agent like Snow."

My gaze leveled on Emma, trying to find her in those shadows. I saw only darkness. Raped. I couldn't imagine such a thing. I'd had sex more times than I should have, had been too young, unprepared, doing it for all the wrong reasons, but each time had been my decision. I didn't know how I would have reacted if I'd been forced.

I wanted to go to her, but didn't. She'd only push me away, reject me. I knew it beyond any doubt. Besides, what help could I give her? I didn't know the pain of what she'd endured; in her mind, I'd never be able to understand. It was like a nonuser trying to talk to me about addiction. Nothing came of it but frustration.

Just then, someone laughed. Someone else chortled. I tore my attention from the corner and scanned the room again. Nothing had changed. Conversation flowed around us like rivers.

The older girls preferred the lounge area, I realized after closer inspection. They kept most of the boys occupied—except for a small group who stood off to the side, gazing wide-eyed at everything around them. Exactly like me and my friends were doing.

They must be the new male recruits.

"Which one do you think is that perv Bradley?" Kitten asked, leaning into me.

"Oh, oh, oh. And just who is Bradley?" Cara twirled a lock of dark hair around her finger. "Where'd you meet him?"

"Yeah," Jenn piped in, her expression rapt. "Tell us!"

Kitten quickly explained, and she couldn't keep the relish from her voice.

"Maybe that one's Bradley," Dani said, pointing. She was pretty, her pale hair, pale skin, and green eyes giving her a fairy-tale aura as she next waved at one of the boys, grinning coyly.

I looked over at the circle of boys, who were looking at us now. They were all tall and lean and very toned. They ranged in hair color, from the darkest of night to the brightest of morning. A few were gorgeous, some were cute, and the rest had average faces that could easily get lost in a crowd. It was the most handsome one who was waving back at Dani.

"I sincerely hope that's not Bradie boy," I said. Kitten would not like it if Bradley developed a crush on Dani. But as cocky as Bradley was, he had to be one of the gorgeous ones.

I, as it turned out, was wrong.

Two of the boys disconnected from their group and maneuvered through the crowd, heading straight for us. One was plain-looking, and one had a rugged appeal nothing female could deny. Both appeared happy. Cara and Jenn fiddled with their hair and blotted their faces with their hands.

"Testosterone alert," Dani muttered, sounding pleased. Excited.

"Ohmygod, I want him," Cara said. "I call dibs on the tall one."

When the boys arrived, they stopped in front of Kitten. The shorter of the two, the plain one, had dark hair and almost feminine green eyes; he gave the Teran a chin nod. "You Kitten?" he asked.

Instantly I recognized his voice. It was all Bradley: cocky and just a little wicked.

"That's me," Kitten replied. As eager as she'd been to see Bradley at last, she acted nonchalant now. "And you are?"

I wanted to grin, but didn't let myself.

He rolled his eyes, totally unimpressed with Kitten's performance. "As if you don't know, baby. This is my roommate and fellow badass, Erik Trinity. He's in his second semester here." His arm wrapped around Erik's wide shoulders.

Erik had brown hair (that was a little shaggy) and green eyes fringed by long, thick lashes. He radiated confidence and attitude, and something about him beckoned and held a girl's gaze. He was tall and strong, the kind of guy you wanted at your side, who looked like he would stop at nothing to protect you.

"Which one is Phoenix?" Bradley asked.

"That would be me." I raised my hand and gave a finger wave. I should have been excited to meet boys my own age. Especially since Erik was amazingly sexy and was grinning at me as if he wouldn't mind getting to know me.

He wasn't my instructor, and he wasn't strictly forbidden to me. So I should have smiled back. But . . .

"Meet our friends," I said, then introduced them to the others. Erik spotted Cara, who'd called dibs, and his breath caught in his throat.

His smile widened, and a wicked gleam filled his emerald eyes. "Hey."

Fickle, much? I thought with an inward laugh.

Cara twirled a strand of hair. "Hey yourself."

Despite the rules, hookups were going to happen. That much was obvious. Had Ryan hooked up with a fellow student when he'd been in training? The thought had my hands clenching.

Had he ever broken the rules and dated—kissed—a trainee?

Would he?

He would know what he was doing in bed, I thought, and perhaps even be able to give me an orgasm. I was embarrassed to admit it, but as many boys as I'd been with I'd never experienced one. I'd read about it in books, my friends had talked about it, and yet it had always eluded me.

An image of Ryan lying in my bed, summoning me over with a crook of his finger, flashed before my eyes. I shivered. I'd walk over to him, crawl up his body, and he'd kiss the breath right out of me.

"How you likin' your stay here, ladies?" Bradley asked, drawing me away from such bad, bad thoughts.

"I'm not a lady, but I'm suddenly loving it," Erik said.

Everyone chuckled.

"You wanna go get a drink or something?" Bradley asked Kitten.

"No, thanks," she answered. She flipped her multicolored hair over her shoulder. I caught a glimpse of pointed ears. "I'm not thirsty."

Still playing hard to get, was she?

Disappointment flashed over Bradley's freckled face, but he quickly recovered. "Whatever," he said. "You're probably boring, anyway, and would have ruined my good time."

"Boring!" she gasped, glaring up at him.

"That's right." He leaned into her personal space. "Your ears are working fine. I said boring. Want me to spell it, too?"

"You wanting me to scratch out your eyes and eat them?"

He flashed a smug grin. "Still desperate for a piece of me, are you?"

"Why you little—"

"Come on, Erik," he said, cutting her off. "I need a shot of caffeine to wake me up. Kitten almost put me to sleep." Without another word, the two boys were off. Bradley practically had to drag poor Erik, though, who kept throwing glances at Cara over his shoulder.

"I'll kill him," Kitten growled. "Kill him!"

"Why didn't you have a drink with him?" Cara demanded, stomping her foot. "I wasn't done talking to Erik."

"If Erik had wanted to talk to you, girlie, he would have stayed," Kitten bit out. Her eyes watched Bradley as he approached another group of girls. She hissed under her breath. "A player. I knew it. And I am not boring!"

"Why don't you just admit it. You wanted a piece of Bradley," I said.

She snorted and turned away from the boys. "As if."

I shook my head—and from the corner of my eye I spotted Ryan standing in the doorway. I gulped. "Uh, listen, I need a moment . . . away from the crowd."

"Want me to come with?"

"Nah." Just seeing him for that brief second, my blood was too hot. My limbs were shaky. My airways were constricted. "Stay here. Have fun. I'll be back soon." As I walked to the door, I saw that he was gone. Where was he?

I stepped out, searching . . . searching . . .

"Not your kind of party?"

Gasping, I straightened. He stepped from the shadows. Seeing him again, I actually ached. "Going to the party?"

"No. Not my turn to chaperone." He paused. His head tilted to the side as he studied me. "Want to walk with me? Talk?"

Not a question that needed consideration. I nodded and stepped to his side. His pine scent hit me, and his hand brushed mine. Goose bumps broke out over my skin. I should have been used to them by now. We started forward, the only two people in the hall.

Why did the things that were wrong always feel so good?

"What do you want to talk about?" I asked to fill the silence.

"Why don't you tell me about your last boyfriend," he said, eyes remaining straight ahead.

I almost choked. No way did I want to discuss my stupid decisions. "Why don't you tell me about your last girlfriend?"

His shoulders lifted in a shrug. "We didn't last long. She was a civilian and resented all the time I spent here. Your turn."

Fine. "He was four years older than me. I met him in rehab, but he hadn't been ready to stop using. I almost let him convince me to fly again—just one more. One more. Yeah, right."

Mom said I went for older boys because I was looking for a father figure. Anything to make up for the way my dad had abandoned us. But surely I was smarter now. Wiser.

That's why I'm crushing on Ryan, huh? Because I'm smarter?

"You didn't use, though," he said, "and that's what's important."

183

"Not dating losers is equally important, but I ignored that little bit of wisdom."

Ryan chuckled. We hit the end of the hallway and turned around, heading back to the party. "What's been your favorite part of camp so far?"

Honestly? "Your class." The demonstration, to be precise.

"You sucking up to the teacher?"

"If I wanted to suck up to the teacher, I wouldn't have punched him in the face."

His grin widened. "True."

Though we'd slowed our steps, we reached the doors all too soon. I wanted to go again, but he said, "Phoenix," and stopped. Looked at me. "You still unsure about staying?"

I gazed down at my boots. "I'd like to stay, but I feel like everyone's just waiting to kick me out." I couldn't help myself; I moved closer to him. He didn't back away. So badly I wanted to kiss him, and I didn't care about the rules. I just wanted his tongue in my mouth.

But as we looked at each other, a trio of boys laughingly stumbled from the room. Ryan and I jumped guiltily apart. Would he have let me? If we hadn't been interrupted, would he have let me kiss him?

"If you're going to get kicked out, it's always better to go down fighting," he said, backing away. "It's better to be the one they regret and miss and wonder about than the one they're confident in losing."

"Maybe."

"Definitely."

Disappointment rocked me that he was leaving. "See you around." He nodded, spun on his heel, and strode off.

"Better to go down fighting," he'd said. The thought of giving it my all and still failing was frightening. That would be more proof that I was a loser.

Sighing, I shoved open the door and stepped back into the room. The music was just as loud and grinding, and my friends had remained where I'd left them. They smiled as I rejoined them.

"Hey, Phoenix," a hard voice suddenly said.

"Yes." I sent my gaze to the speaker. She stood to my left. She was a pretty girl with dark hair, dark eyes. Pissed expression. Allison Stone. Ryan's sister.

"I heard you took Ryan down yesterday," she said. Her gaze sparkled with challenge.

"Yeah. So?" She'd made her dislike of me clear during my interview, so I wasn't going to waste my time being nice to her. "What are you doing at a party for trainees?"

She grinned with relish. "I'm the chaperone."

Six of her friends lined up beside her. They crossed their arms over their chests one after the other. "So," Allison said with a smug edge, "I think you think you're better than us."

"Think? Good one." Kitten moved to my side. She studied her elongated claws and purred low in her throat. "I don't know where you get your info, but you're wrong. She doesn't think it; she knows it. *We* know it."

Fury blazed over Allison's features. "Why don't you prove it, then, weakling?" She reached out and pushed me.

I stumbled backward a few steps. When I righted, I ran my tongue over my teeth. *Oh, no, no, no.* We weren't going to play this game. There would be no pushing me around. But fighting with her wasn't an option. It was against the rules. I could be kicked out. She wouldn't. Boss was her dad. I bet Allison could murder me and not get in trouble. Still.

If I let her intimidate me now, she would continue to do so. Her friends, too. I'd seen it a thousand times, and I admit, I'd done it to others. I had to prove myself now or suffer for the rest of the year.

I had to try to make her back down. But could I do it without breaking a single rule?

"You touch me again," I said, eyes narrowed, lips pulled tight, "and I'll make you sorry."

Her mouth curled in a smug smile. Smug, smug, smug. Everything about her was smug. "That's highly doubtful. I've had nearly twelve months of training. I can take little girls like you and snap your necks."

I closed every inch of space between us. Our noses touched. Her breath blended with mine. Around me I heard conversations taper to quiet. My heartbeat quickened. I knew I was outmatched. I'd seen her fighting skills when she'd battled the Sybilins. And I knew I'd gotten lucky when I overpowered Ryan yesterday. He hadn't expected me to act. Allison, though, expected it. Wanted it.

But again, I couldn't back down, couldn't show any hint of fear.

I raised my chin. "Go ahead and try it. I'll do to you what I did to that Sybilin: punch your face into powder."

A little color drained from her face. Good. She remembered that I, too, had some skills, raw though they were. But she didn't back down, either. "All you are is a druggie. A burned-out, stupid flyer."

I heard several people gasp. My jaw clenched. How dare she tell them about my past. How dare she! That was privileged information. Too late to keep it quiet now. "I'm a *former* flyer who isn't afraid of you."

"You don't deserve to be here, former user or not. You're not good enough."

"Your daddy thought differently." I paused, forced an evil smile. "Is that why *you're* here? Did Daddy pull some strings?"

Her eyes darkened, and I saw her decision to attack solidify there. I owed the observation to Le'Ace. Because of her, I was learning to watch and absorb details that I had never noticed before.

Allison swung at me, her open palm flying toward my nose. She meant to slam the cartilage into my brain. Bitch. Ryan had showed me this move in class—and exactly what to do. Rather than shoulder her in the stomach, however, I ducked and kicked out my leg, bouncing her ankles together and sending her toppling to the ground.

She gasped in shock, in disbelief, but was back on her feet before I could blink. A moment later, she fisted me in the cheek. This time, I didn't have time to dodge. At contact, my head whipped to the side. Pain exploded in my head.

Adrenaline swam through me, thick and potent, thankfully drowning all hint of pain. In seconds, I was so high on it, I felt stronger than ever before. Invincible. Powerful.

I ducked as she swung again and punched her in the stomach. The fight was on now. Air whooshed from her mouth. She bent over, jerking me down with her. Then we were on the ground, rolling, rolling, until she was on top of me. Using all my newfound strength, I bucked her off, pinned her down, and punched her in the face—just as I'd promised.

"Bitch," she growled, and we rolled for a second time. She knifed her pointed fingers toward my throat. "My brother is not for you!"

I managed to grip her wrist before contact, stopping her momentum. "I never said he was." I arched my back and bucked again, dislodging her just enough to twist one of my legs up and kick toward her stomach.

Before I made contact, someone caught me from behind in an iron-clad grip. "Stop! What the hell do you think you're doing?"

Ryan.

His voice echoed in my ears. I whipped to face him just as

Allison pounded forward. She leapt into the air, spun, and meant to knock me in the face with her foot. She would have done it, too, but before I knew what he was doing, Ryan twisted us and took the blow himself.

Allison fell to the ground, gasping, "Ryan! Ryan, I'm sorry." Contrite, she rushed to his side.

Everyone paused and watched what was going on between brother and sister. And me, the outsider. Who knows what they were thinking. *I* didn't know what to think.

Fury contorting his face, Ryan pointed a finger in Allison's face. "You know better, Al. You know better than to act this way." His lip was bleeding, already swelling. "Go see Boss. He's waiting for you in his office."

She hesitated, paled. Her expression was tortured as she looked from Ryan to me, me to Ryan.

"Go!" he commanded harshly.

She spun and fled from the room.

"You," he said, grabbing hold of me once more. "Come with me." Without waiting for my reply, he tugged me into the hall, following the same path Allison had taken.

I could feel the anger radiating from him. There was something else, though, something I couldn't name that drifted beneath the negative emotion. I tossed a helpless glance over my shoulder and connected with Kitten's gaze. One of her eyes was already black and she was panting, but she smiled at me, a contented cat.

A set of doors closed, blocking out her image.

Ryan stopped, turned on me, and pointed a finger in my face, just as he'd done to his sister. "What the hell was that about?"

I crossed my arms over my chest and cast my gaze throughout our surroundings. We were in the hall, and we were alone. "Ask Allison," I said. "*She* came to *me* looking for trouble."

He arched a brow, not pacified in the least. "My sister has never attacked another trainee before. Did you provoke her?"

Scowling, I slapped at his finger. A few minutes ago, he'd been super nice to me, so his accusation hurt all the more. "I. Did. Nothing. So don't you dare try to blame this on me."

He grabbed my wrist. I thought he meant to jerk me forward and scream in my face for daring to hit him, but he didn't. He held onto me, stared at the length of my arm. Bit by bit, his expression softened. "You have talent, Phoenix. I don't want to see it wasted."

My shoulders sagged, the fire of my anger dying a quick death. Our gazes met, exactly as they had only a short while ago. A shiver of awareness stole over me. I drank in his appeal. I could feel his body heat. His fingers were calloused and created a dizzying friction against my skin.

In the next instant, he released me and stepped away. He tangled a hand in his dark hair. "What are you doing to me?"

My jaw dropped in astonishment. "Me? I'm not doing anything." *Except wanting you,* I added silently. I still wanted him to kiss me. The need was so strong that I suddenly didn't care about being kicked out. About getting in trouble and having my memory wiped.

"Not doing anything—ha!" He snorted. Once again, he closed the distance between us.

Yes, I thought. Closer . . . closer . . .

His clean, pine scent wafted around me. "You're all I can think about anymore," he whispered in my ear. "I look for you in the halls. I'm constantly wondering what you're doing and who you're doing it with. Why do you think I was looking in on the party? I was hoping you'd catch a glimpse of me and come out. I can't get you out of my mind, even though you're forbidden."

I gulped. So, he felt it, too, then. The hum of attraction. The need. I opened my mouth to reply, to tell him how I felt, but he shook his head.

"Don't say a damn word," he said in that whisper. "If I hear that you want me, too, I'll lose control." He pushed out a shaky breath, and it fanned my lobe. "Boss watched your fight. He watches and sees everything because there are cameras everywhere. Even here."

I paled.

"Come on," Ryan said, loudly this time. "Boss wants to see you and Allison."

I followed behind him, staring at his back. His words replayed through my mind. Not that words that should have, but the ones that shouldn't have: You're all I can think about anymore.

Ryan wanted me. Ryan really wanted me!

A wonderful and terrible discovery. For a few, needy seconds, I had thought I could give up A.I.R. for a single kiss from him. Lucid now, I knew that wasn't true. I couldn't. I wouldn't.

I belonged here. I didn't want to leave, no matter what I had to do to remain.

The knowledge swam inside me as if a switch had been thrown. I admitted it now—now that I'd broken a rule and being kicked out was more a possibility than ever. A bitter laugh escaped me. What a time to realize the truth. This camp *was* worth fighting with all my might to stay.

I had purpose here. I had goals. Becoming an A.I.R. agent was forever; protecting innocents was honorable. There was no better career choice for me. *I can't lose this.*

At the moment, camp was all I had.

I remained silent while Ryan led me through the halls. Soon I found myself seated across from Allison and facing the silver-haired Boss, who sat behind a large desk. He wore those same black glasses. The entire wall behind him was sectioned into different holoscreens, displaying different scenes. The party. All the classrooms, which were currently empty. The hallways. Kids who were striding to and from their rooms.

Boss leaned back and crossed his arms over his chest. "Someone want to tell me what that was about?" he asked in that deep voice of his.

I shrugged, trying to act nonchalant even though fear pounded through me. This was exactly the situation I hadn't wanted to find myself in. *Thanks a lot, Allison.*

My knuckles throbbed as I came down from my adrenaline high.

"She's a bitch," Allison said, pointing at me.

I didn't respond, though I wanted to. Badly. *Hold it together; act like an agent.*

"You've been against her since Ryan told me how she fought and Mia recommended her," Boss said. "Why?"

"She's a flyer," Allison gritted out.

"Former," I said.

"Flyers do not recover," Allison insisted. "Especially not this one. You didn't see her in school, Dad. She used Breathless constantly. She was rude. She stole things from my locker. She treated everyone but her friends like dirt. She was loud and obnoxious in class, always disrupting the teacher. Some of us actually wanted to learn," she snapped at me.

My hands fisted. "*She* finally got clean. *She* hasn't used in months. *She* even passed Angel's test. *She* is also sorry for stealing from you." I'd stolen a lot of things, I knew that, but I didn't remember what or from who.

"Will you be able to resist when we're in the field and drugs are all around you?" Allison demanded. "You'll get high and the rest of us will be left vulnerable because of it."

I raised my chin, determined. "You haven't even given me a chance. You've already held my trial and convicted me."

"She's right," Boss said, gaze narrowed on his daughter.

Allison's lips pressed together in a tight line, but she didn't comment.

"This is strike one, girls. Two more and you're out. And yes, Allison, I'm talking to you, as well. For today's incident, I'm forbidding both of you from attending social functions for two weeks. If you fight again, the consequences will be worse. I need my trainees to work together, to be a team. If there's friction among agents, other-worlders will exploit it and win. That's why you will now spend a few hours every evening together, getting to know each other."

"What!" Allison gasped.

Boss arched his brows, and they peeked over the top rim of his sunglasses. I was surprised to see that his eyebrows were inky black. "I've given my final verdict. You may leave."

Pause.

We sat in stunned disbelief. For different reasons, I'm sure.

"Leave!" he barked.

Neither of us spoke a word as we stood. We glanced at each other, frowned, then looked away. Two weeks of Allison. I didn't like it, but I'd endure it. I hadn't been cut from the program. Not severe as he'd promised.

I was grinning as I left.

12

Surprisingly, the next two weeks passed with lightning speed, my forced time with Allison the only dark spot. I was tested for Onadyn every day, and I passed. I loved my new friends. I loved my classes and was learning so much.

Well, that wasn't exactly true. I should have been learning so much. I was having trouble memorizing the minute details. There were just *so* many species and so much information to take in that I sometimes found myself daydreaming during class.

Sometimes I prayed for the proverbial bell to ring.

So far I'd learned that some aliens didn't breathe from their noses, but from their ears. Some didn't have a spinal cord or bones or even heartbeats. Some excreted poison and we weren't to touch them. Could I name which aliens had these traits? No. Not even upon threat of death.

Really, how was a girl supposed to keep all of that straight?

Of course, there was one thing I knew for certain. I missed my interaction with Ryan. I saw him in combat class, but he never again called me up to demonstrate. He never made eye contact with me. After the amazing things he'd said to me . . . he wanted me, he thought about me constantly . . . I was going crazy.

Logically, I knew why he was treating me this way. Logically, I knew it was better that way. But I didn't like it and I wanted him to stop.

Don't think about him. I need to study! We were going to be tested soon. Okay. So. The Arcadians were psychics, superfast, and almost humanoid.

The Mecs, I'd discovered, could control the weather and liked things hot. The best way to weaken them was to freeze them. Artic, a gun that shot bullets of liquid nitrogen, was in development. I couldn't wait to try it!

Ell Rollises, who were large and strong but could not form a thought on their own, were often used as bodyguards. They obeyed orders without hesitation and when they were given a task, nothing deterred them from it. Even if those orders were to destroy the world.

Some Tarens—Kitten's race—could actually walk through walls. Kitten denied having the ability herself and refused to confirm that others like her actually could. She refused to confirm *anything*. I was glad she'd remained mute. I mean, really. Learning that I (and others) could incapacitate my roommate and friend by pinching the back of her neck had not been fun.

I didn't feel sorry for Kitten, though. We were also learning how to incapacitate humans in case they interfered with our work.

In weapons class, I'd finally gotten to fire a loaded pyregun. The beam shot from the barrel smoothly, easily. In fact, I wouldn't have known I'd fired if not for the yellow beam that had lit up the room like a fireworks display. Well, that and the aftereffects. The destruction from that beam was amazing. My target had become a smoldering pile of ash in seconds.

My strength, I had learned, was in my aim. The more I practiced, the better I became. I was very, very good at hitting what I focused on, even from long distances. I could throw shooting stars better than anyone in my class.

Ryan had taught us how to hide and eject razors from our shoes and shirtsleeves. Every day I felt a little more powerful. A little more important. A little more unbeatable. I think I'd wanted to feel that way my entire life, but hadn't, and so had turned to Onadyn to forget my failure. A.I.R. was my new high.

I grinned. What's more, once a week we practiced breaking and entering. So far, we'd learned how to tap phones and bypass a general security system. How cool was that?

"What are you smiling about?" Allison snipped.

I quickly lost my grin. The two of us usually spent our time griping and insulting each other. Today, our last day together, was apparently not going to be different.

"Mind your own business," I said.

"Mind your own business," she mocked.

I flipped her off and sat back in the uncomfortable chair I'd been assigned. I stared up at the ceiling, knowing cameras were watching me. I didn't know where they were, though, because the ceiling looked like any other. Blocked and silver. Unassuming.

"This sucks," I muttered.

"I'd rather eat maggots than be here with you."

"Maybe I'll talk to your dad about arranging that for you."

"Talk to him and I'll kill you." Her fists clenched atop the table that separated us. "One day, we're going to meet on the streets and—"

"Let me guess," I said, cutting into her speech. "You'll make me sorry I was ever born. Very original."

She didn't reply, and I forced my mind away from her. God knows I'd rather think about anything but her—even my upcoming math exam. Math. Ugh. I almost groaned.

I'd found out that I had passed all my regular studies tests but math. Therefore, I had to take a math class every night. Trig, of all things. Why hadn't that been deemed obsolete by now? Once I passed that, I'd get to graduate high school. I was excited by that prospect. Me, a graduate!

I'd written my mom about it, but had not heard back. Either she hadn't written or A.I.R. was screening my mail (as promised). I was hoping the latter. My therapy sessions with

Angel convinced me more every day that my mom did care about me, she just didn't know how to deal with the thought of losing me like she'd lost my father.

I know I'd thought it before, but one day I really was going to make her proud of me. I was going to apologize for every negative thing I'd ever done to her. I was going to pay her bills and let her retire, relax, and enjoy life. That was my dream, at least. No one had told me how much money A.I.R. agents raked in. But even if I made a pittance, every dime would go to her.

Bad daughter no more. Nope, not me. I was someone to praise.

I mean, I sat through my boring alien politics class every Wednesday and I didn't punch the walls or allow myself to fall asleep—even though I sometimes wanted to sleep more than anything else in the world because I still hadn't adjusted to my new schedule. Now that was discipline!

Really, who cared about the ruling classes of the other-worlders? I didn't.

I'd much rather be in my Thursday alien interrogation class. Now that was a class guaranteed to keep a girl up at night. In it, we learned exactly what to say and do to get the answers we needed. Through unassuming questions at first, we were to discover what the subject wanted or was afraid of and then use that information to our advantage. We were to maintain eye contact. We were to lie. We were also to torture, if necessary, to get what we wanted.

I shuddered at the thought, an action born of dread and anticipation. Keeping this planet safe was as heady as it was scary.

"What are you thinking about now?" Allison demanded.

"Torture," I answered honestly.

One of her eyebrows quirked up. "Mine?"

I shrugged. "Perhaps."

"That's not something I'll ever have to worry about. You'll be kicked out of camp sooner or later. You and that Teran friend of yours."

"She has a name," I said through clenched teeth.

"Yeah. Alien."

I gripped my knees to keep from reaching out and slapping her. "She's a better person than you'll ever be." Kitten and I had grown very close these last two weeks. She was, without a doubt, my best friend here.

She hadn't cared about my drug use. She was smart and witty and always had my back. At school, I'd had friends but they would have ratted me out to save themselves—and often had. I also loved that Kitten was as crazy for Bradley as I was for Ryan. Not that either of us would ever admit to such a thing. Well, not out loud.

Every night I got to hear a replay on the "awful" things Bradley said to Kitten at their last encounter.

"Why don't you find someone else?" I'd finally asked her yesterday.

"Because," had been her stubborn response. "And who said I wanted him?"

I had rolled my eyes. "If you don't want him, tell him that. Maybe he'll leave you alone and find someone else."

She'd hissed low in her throat. "He just smells so good, okay. But I don't share, ever, and he's the type who likes to spread it around."

Unlike us, Cara and Erik had copped to feelings. During the mixers, they were always hiding in a corner, talking, laughing, and touching each other. I sighed, a little jealous.

"What now?" Allison said.

"Why do you want to know?"

"Your voice is better than silence. Slightly," she added darkly.

"Yours isn't," I replied. God, I wanted to shake her. She was so smug, so superior. And I was still fuming about her disdain for Kitten.

Allison scowled over at me. "Listen. Let's cut the crap and talk about the real issue here. You like my brother. I see the way you look at him, and I'm sick of it."

I chewed on the inside of my cheek until the metallic twang of blood lined my tongue. "Well, do you see the way he looks at me?"

"He doesn't like you," she insisted. She leaned forward, palms resting on the table. "And even if he did, he wouldn't risk our father's wrath and do something about it. The two of you are hopeless."

I knew that, and I didn't like the reminder. "If we're hopeless, why are you so worked up about it?"

She ran her tongue over her lips, but didn't say anything.

"Nothing's going to happen between us, okay," I said, bitterness layering my words. "So you can just relax about it."

"Fine."

"Fine."

She turned her head, staring at the walls that enclosed us. Several minutes ticked by. The silence became thick and heavy, enveloping us.

"What do you think everyone is doing right now?" she asked. For the first time, she spoke to me as if I were an acquaintance rather than an enemy.

"Having fun," I grumbled.

"Yeah," she said wistfully. "Having fun."

It was Friday, social day, so everyone was at a party. They were drinking punch, eating delicious food; they were talking and laughing. And I was stuck here. New hookups were probably happening right now. I wondered if Bradley and Kitten had finally made a move on each other.

"You know," Allison said on a long sigh, "I never got in trouble before you arrived."

"So I've been told," I said dryly. "You shouldn't have attacked me. Why did you, anyway? And don't say your brother—you knew nothing would ever happen between us."

"You were getting on my nerves, strutting around as if you owned the place." She drew a circle on the tabletop. "I've been here for months. Me. Not you. I've earned the right to strut. You haven't."

That wasn't the only reason she'd jumped me. I could see the knowledge in her eyes. "I'd say it was to solidify your place here, but you've been here so long, you don't need to prove yourself anymore."

"Ha! You have no idea."

I sat up straighter in my chair, peering at her. "Then why don't you explain it to me so that I *do* understand?"

Her jaw became a mutinous line a split second before she crumbled and the words poured from her. "I always have to prove myself. My father runs this place. If I'm not the best, people begin to question my talent, as if I don't have any. They forget the kills I've already made."

I arched a brow, a mimic of the expression she'd given me a little while ago. A mimic of her father. "So you decided to challenge me? A new trainee?"

"Everyone's in awe of you." She scrubbed a hand down her face. "Did you see the new girl?" she said, sotto voce. "I hear she took down a gang of Sybilins on her own. Did you see the new girl? I hear she knocked Ryan on his ass."

I wanted to grin at the memory, but didn't dare. There was a vulnerability to Allison now that kind of—God, I hated to admit this—saddened me. Even reminded me of myself.

"I have to prove myself, too, you know?" I told her.

She snorted in disbelief. "Everyone already loves you."

"I'm the girl who was addicted to Onadyn. I'm the girl

who could start flying again at any moment. I'm the girl the instructors might kick out at any moment." I crossed my arms over my chest, daring her to contradict me.

Her cheeks fused with color, a bright, bright red. "All right. Fine. You have to prove yourself, too."

A few seconds later, a buzzer announced the end of our session. Neither one of us stood right away. We just looked at each other.

"I'm sorry I jumped you," she said grudgingly.

I hadn't expected an apology, even though we'd reached a sort of truce, and I was momentarily rendered speechless. "Well, uh, I'm sorry you jumped me, too."

Her lips edged into a smile; it was the first she'd ever given me. "You have an attitude problem, you know that?"

I felt my own lips curling upward. "Maybe we were separated at birth."

She laughed out loud this time, amusement lighting her entire face, softening her, making her a beautiful sight. She stood. "See you around, Phoenix."

"Yeah. See you around, Allison."

She strode from the room with the cocky swagger of an agent. Not a trainee, but an actual agent. I had to admire her for that. I pushed to my feet, too. With a sigh, I left the "naughty" room, as I'd come to call it.

I ground to a halt the moment I stepped into the hall, though. Emma was leaning against the wall, her hands in her pockets. Her pale hair was in disarray around her shoulders, and there were shadows under her eyes. The trident tattooed on her cheek seemed larger than before. Maybe because her cheeks were a bit sunken.

I'd always wondered why she'd gotten that tattoo and what it meant.

"Hey," I said. Each day during anatomy class, I'd invited her to my room later that day to study. Each day, she'd ignored me.

"Hey," she replied, staring down at her boots.

Well, well, well. Today was a day of firsts, I guess. Allison and I had walked away on easy terms, and now Emma was speaking to me. "What are you doing here? Why aren't you at the party?"

She met my gaze briefly. "I needed to talk to you."

"About what?" I didn't ask with heat; I asked with genuine curiosity.

She pulled her hands from her pockets and twisted them together. "My aim sucks. No matter what I do, I can't make it better."

When she said no more, I prompted, "And?"

"And yours doesn't suck."

Realization dawned, and I nodded. "You want my help." A statement, not a question.

She nodded, the action stiff.

A moment passed as I considered my answer. Finally I said, "I'll make you a deal. You help me study alien anatomy, and I'll help you with your aim."

She answered quickly, with no hesitation, as if I'd given her exactly what she'd hoped for. "Deal."

"Want to start now? I've got time."

She lifted her shoulders in a nonchalant shrug, but I could see the eagerness in her eyes.

"Come on."

We walked side-by-side to the arena. After an ID scan, the doors opened and we swept inside. Because of the party, I didn't expect anyone to be here. But Siren was firing at a target and when she spotted us, she stilled. She sheathed the pyre-gun at her side and faced us.

She wasn't as pretty as the other women of A.I.R, but her red hair was amazing. It hung down her shoulders like a silky curtain. "Here to practice?" she asked in that oh so sweet voice of hers.

We nodded. I hadn't seen her since my first day and I couldn't help but remember that she hadn't wanted me here. "Too much attitude," she'd said. A part of me wanted to show her *real* attitude, the kind that came with five fingers and an equal number of knuckles.

"That makes me proud. That makes me proud." She strode from the room with a grin.

I watched her, frowning, confused. O-kay. Not what I had expected. "You'll always suck," maybe. Or, "You shouldn't be here, you drugged-out loser."

I shook my head, strangely happy. "Let's get started," I said to Emma. I collected a pyre-gun with no detonation crystal since we weren't allowed to hold a loaded gun without Kadar's presence, as well as a few sharp-edged stars from the glass case.

The computer logged my ID before permitting me to handle a single weapon, keeping a list of everything I took. If any of those items were not returned or were used on someone, I would be blamed. If I tried to leave the room with them, alarms would erupt and, I was sure, any instructor nearby would tackle or shoot me.

"Line up," I told Emma.

She approached the open window that looked onto the jelly molds and holograms of the aliens. In a hologram, we could change the race of the alien with a few clicks of a keyboard—only during our free time, however. In class, Kadar picked for us. Emma changed the Delensean hologram to a . . .

"What is that?" I asked her, studying the shiny, light blue creature with the webbed hands and feet.

Her expression hardened. "It's a Lyross."

I'd heard that name before. Where? I flipped through my mental files, and my eyes widened as realization struck. The Lyross, a race that lived underwater. The race of her rapist. "Stars or, uh, guns?"

"Stars first. Guns second."

I set the gun aside and stood behind her, reaching around to grasp her wrist.

The moment I touched her, she jumped and jerked away

from me. She struggled for breath as she faced me, her features pale. "What do you think you're doing?"

"Easy," I said, palms up. "I'm just correcting your aim."

"I don't like it when people are behind me."

I should have realized that. "I'm not going to hurt you, Emma, and you're just going to have to take my word on that if you want my help."

She gulped, and several minutes passed before she relaxed her shoulders inch by inch. Finally she turned, facing her target.

Slowly I approached her and wrapped my arms around her. She stiffened, but didn't move away this time. "You want to hold the star gently. Like this. With your fingers here, here, and here."

"That can't be right." She flicked me a scowl. "I've held it like this before and I missed the target every time."

"Just bare with me." I positioned her arm, with her elbow slightly bent. "Get your target in sight, then throw, rotating your wrist forward as you launch."

She nodded, her gaze never leaving the hologram of the Lyross. There was hate in her eyes. As I guided her arm backward and forward, keeping my fingertips on the bend of her wrist, she tossed the star and it cut right into the Lyross's crotch.

Ouch. I cringed.

She laughed, and the sound was joyous. "I did it. I really did it!"

I found myself grinning. "See. It's all in the wrist."

"I want to do it again." Her amusement became dark, almost evil. "By myself, this time."

Should I be concerned by that? I wondered, but handed her another star. She turned to the Lyross, lined up, and threw. Without my aid, the sharp metal sailed over its shoulder. "Damn it!"

"Your wrist was stiff. Try again. But relax, like before."

We stayed there for more than an hour, throwing one star after another. We never even got to the gun. It proved to be a workout and by the end we were sweating. She'd thrown as if she were slaying her biggest nightmare. But she was hitting more than she missed now, so it was worth it.

When we paused to catch our breath, I finally asked about her tattoo. "Why a trident? And why on your face." Most girls would have gotten a rose or a butterfly on their back or ankle.

A long while passed before she answered. "You heard the story of Poseidon?" she asked. We sat across from each other, leaning against the wall.

"He's god of the sea, right?"

She nodded.

And that's when the truth hit me. Poseidon. Underwater. Lyross.

"In myth Poseidon punishes someone with his trident. There's unimaginable power in it. So to me, the trident means vengeance. As to why it's on my face . . ." Her shoulders lifted in another of those deceptively casual shrugs. "I like to look at it. I like to be reminded that vengeance will one day be mine."

My heart ached for her. To live with that kind of hate . . . it was one of the things that had driven me to Onadyn. I hoped she learned to control it before it controlled her. "I know what happened to you," I said softly, "and I want you to know—"

"You don't know shit," she growled, cutting me off.

"Yes, Emma, I do." I peered over at her. "You were raped."

Dark storm clouds seemed to envelop her, and she jumped to her feet. Our easy camaraderie was destroyed. "How do you know that? Who told you that?"

I stood, too. "Emma, it's okay."

"It's okay? Did you just say that it's okay?"

"Yes."

She sucked in a deep, shuddering gulp of air. "I did nothing wrong. But do you like your shame talked about, Phoenix? Do you like knowing that people know your darkest secret?" She didn't give me a chance to respond. "Who else knows?"

"Ev— everyone in our class," I admitted.

She laughed, the sound completely devoid of humor. "Some backup team you guys are. You're supposed to build me up, not tear me down. And now I find out that you've been talking about me behind my back. Thanks a lot." Her chin was trembling as she spun around and ran.

"Emma," I called, but she didn't slow. I'd meant to help

her, to express my sympathy and try to make her feel better. She was right, though. I hated it when people discussed my past.

I scrubbed a hand down my face. *Way to go, Phoenix. Way to go.*

Not wanting to be alone, I headed to the party. Surprisingly, I ran into Ryan along the way. We were the only two people in the hallway and I had to wonder if we were being tested.

Our gazes locked. He nodded as he passed me, our shoulders brushing. I shivered, and he sucked in a breath. But we never spoke. I couldn't help but experience a rush of disappointment.

At the mixer, I found myself alone—just as I hadn't wanted to be. Everyone was already paired off and things had wound down. Then Cara, who was laughing at something Erik said, spotted me and motioned me over.

Did I want to remain alone or become a third wheel? Not really needing to think about it, I clomped to them.

"Hey," she and Erik said in unison. At that, they shared a laugh.

"Hey." I sat in the vacant spot beside them on the couch.

"Heard about your punishment," Erik said. "But you survived, I see."

"Yeah. It was iffy for a while."

He grinned. His arm was wrapped around Cara's shoulders, and he was tracing his fingertips up her arm. Cara leaned her head against him. They looked so in sync. So perfect for each other.

It was kind of sickening.

"Want some punch or something?" he asked me.

"No, thanks." Why couldn't Ryan be that solicitous? "So what have you been up to?"

"The usual." His shoulders lifted in a shrug. "Class, class, and more class. Alien history is a real snoozefest. Rick Townsend actually *did* fall asleep. They made him pack his bags that day. Probably wiped his memory before sending him home, poor bastard."

Wow.

"We've lost three boys already."

I glanced to Cara. So far we hadn't lost anyone. I think, perhaps, it was only a matter of time, though. Jenn didn't have the instinct and if Emma's aim didn't improve on a more regular basis. . . . And if I didn't start obeying the rules . . . "I hate feeling like the ax could drop at any moment, you know?"

"Yeah," he said. "But, hey, if you ever need anything, just let me know. I'd hate to see you go."

What a sweet thing to say. No wonder Cara was wild for him. "Thank you."

He kissed Cara's cheek, detangled from her, and stood. "Bradley's calling me over. Looks like Kitten's about to kill him."

As he walked away, I found myself staring at his back.

He was actually a pretty great guy. The world needed more like him. Hell, maybe Ryan should take boyfriend lessons from him.

Next combat class, I just might suggest it. Maybe that would pull Ryan from his ignore Phoenix phase. Well, a girl could hope.

13

A day that had seemed promising, then disappointing, then promising again gave way to a tension-filled night. Kitten and I were woken up after only two hours of sleep. One second our room lights were out, the next they were beaming brightly.

The computer voice said, "Please rise, Kitten and Phoenix. You have fifteen minutes to prepare for a tour. Meet in room three A."

"A tour?" Kitten grumbled sleepily.

I yawned and rubbed my eyes. When would my internal clock adjust to these midnight hours? "This is cruel and unusual punishment. We're growing kids. We need sleep."

"What kind of tour, do you think?"

"Of the building?"

"Nah. We've seen everything."

"I don't think they'd take us out, though." I hadn't seen

sunlight, or moonlight for that matter, in weeks. Yawning again, I stretched my arms over my head.

Kitten lumbered out of bed and shook my leg. "Get up, sleepy."

"No."

"Up or I'll tell Ryan Stone you *luuuv* him."

Frowning, I slapped at her hand. "Then I'll tell Bradley you want to have his baby. What do you think of that?"

"Ryan and Phoenix," she sang, then she made kissing noises. "Up, up, up."

"Fine," I grumbled. "I'm up. I'm up." I eased into a sitting position.

We had a routine for getting ready. She got the bathroom for five minutes. I got it for the next five, then we did two minutes of running in place to get our blood pumping. So far, the system had worked.

"Think the boys are coming?" she asked as she strode into the shower stall, stripping along the way.

"God, I hope not." They'd only be trouble. Fun, irreverent, and amusing, yes, but mostly trouble. Neither of us concentrated when the boys were around. We needed to start, though, since we'd begin classes with them when we reached the next level of our training.

If we reached it, which I was determined to do.

Dressed in our white shirts and slightly loose white pants (I guess we'd both lost a little weight), we headed to room 3A. The day before, Kitten had ripped the sleeves of her shirt and frayed the hem of her pants, giving the uniform a little personality.

As we jogged down the hall, I tied my top in the middle and rolled the waist of my pants, revealing a thin strip of stomach. Most noticeably, however, was the skull and crossbones I'd drawn on the back of my shirt. I'd had trouble falling asleep, had seen the pen and, well . . . hopefully I wouldn't get in trouble. But how could I? Defacing clothing was *not* mentioned in the rule book.

"I'm sore," Kitten panted. "Already I need a break."

"I just need a bed."

We ran into a few of the other girls along the way: Cara, Lindsay, and Dani. They were a sea of pretty (but tired) faces. Ahead, I saw a door slide open and then Emma was racing from it. Our gazes connected briefly before she looked away.

I wanted to talk to her, to apologize, but now wasn't the time. "Where's Jenn?"

"Didn't you hear? She was booted late last night," Cara said.

Shit! There was a moment of silence as the rest of us absorbed that information. "Why?" I finally asked, though I could guess.

"I wasn't told."

At the entrance to 3A, we all had our hands scanned to prove we were there. Mia Snow was waiting for us inside, and I experienced a wave of déjà vu. The scene was eerily similar to my first night at camp. Only this time I was with friends and I knew what I was doing.

This time I belonged.

I was a part of something greater than myself and the knowledge filled me with pride. Suddenly I wasn't quite so exhausted. I couldn't allow myself to be sent home like Jenn. Poor thing, though she was probably happier.

"Good morning, girls," Mia said. As usual, she wore black syn-leather from neck to ankle. There was a bruise on her chin, as if she'd recently been in a fight. I wanted to ask her about it, but didn't. I'd learned the woman did not like personal questions, and I hadn't yet mastered the fine art of insidious interrogation—getting answers without seeming like I was probing for them.

"What's going on?" I asked. "What kind of tour are we taking?"

"The scary kind." Steps clipped, Mia strode to the door. "Follow me. I'll explain more when we're in the car."

We truly were leaving the building. Wow.

Why, though? Why now?

Mia led us through the hallways, past the classrooms, past the Common, which was empty. Quiet. At the doors that led into the restricted area, she punched in a series of buttons and had her hand scanned.

The doors opened. We stepped into that forbidden hallway, and Kitten whispered, "What did she mean, scary?" Her golden eyes glittered, and her expression lit with excitement.

"Hell if I—know," I finished lamely as I drank in our new surroundings. Unlike the Common, this area pulsed with life. Heavily armed men and women strode in every direction. One man was dragging an unconscious Ell Rollis from one corner to another.

Up close, I could see the alien's dry, yellow skin. Without a nose, its face was grotesque. Its teeth were sharp and protruded over its lips. "What's going on?"

"Business as usual," Mia said.

Kadar passed us next, and he nodded in greeting. "Girls."

"Hi, Kadar," Lindsay said, her voice high and breathless.

Crushing, I guess. When had that happened? Kadar was gorgeous, sure, but I couldn't see him falling for a student. Besides, the man was probably married with three hundred kids. Poor Linds. But, really. Who was I to judge? Queen of the doomed crushes, that was me.

I wasn't even going to think his name.

Le'Ace passed us next. She and Mia pretended not to see each other. The two obviously hated each other, but neither had ever said why.

I'd heard rumors, of course.

According to gossip (not that I listened, *cough, cough*), Le'Ace had stopped aging a long time ago. She'd supposedly been here on and off for over fifty years. Did I believe that? Uh, no. Anyway, Mia had supposedly been a student, one of the more rebellious ones, always making trouble. Did I believe *that*? Uh, yeah. The story went on to say that Le'Ace had been her instructor and had killed one of Mia's friends for purposefully giving the camp's location to an enemy.

That, too, I could believe.

Breathing in the scent of coffee, I forced my attention on the room, memorizing details just as I'd been taught. There were desks and papers, computers and chairs like you'd find in a regular office. Multiple holoscreens and a panel of voice receivers consumed one wall. In my alien biology class, I'd learned that alien voice was similar to human DNA. Their voices contained some sort of frequency ours didn't, outlining their species and gender. And so, recorders were placed all over New Chicago (and the rest of the world) to monitor in case a crime was committed.

I wasn't given a chance to study anything else because we reached the doorway that led outside. A few steps, and I stood just beyond the threshold. That's when I stopped, forgot about the building, and drank in the beauty of the night.

The sky was black velvet with pinpricks of white diamonds. The air was cool and fragrant with man-made lake and pine and dirt. Entranced, I tilted my chin up and splayed my arms. Before coming to this camp, I'd been able to go outside whenever I wanted. I'd lain in the sun for hours, absorbing the warmth; I'd partied in the moonlight, lost in my own little world.

What a difference a few weeks had made. I loved camp, but God, I had missed this. Having my freedom taken away was the absolute worst. I understood the reasoning for it now, might even have accepted it, but that didn't change my frustration at being kept from it.

Kitten gasped, and I turned to see what had startled her. She was facing the building we'd just exited. I turned, too, and blinked in surprise. Uh, there was no building. Only night and dirt.

"A shield covers the building," Mia explained. "It's blocked from the naked eye by modified energy particles."

Tentatively, I reached out. My fingers encountered something jellylike that caused the air around my fingers to dapple and ripple like water. "Wow," I said, awed. "How will we find the door then?"

"You learn." Mia clapped her hands. "Enough chatter. Let's move out. We've got a lot of ground to cover and not a lot of time to do it."

She loaded us inside a large black van—the same van that had brought me here, was my guess. *Sweet memories,* I thought dryly. From the outside, the vehicle appeared completely closed up, no side windows, no doorways. But with a single command of "open" from Mia, two doors popped open.

When we were seated inside, I realized that there were indeed windows; they were simply covered by a shade. Mia claimed the driver's seat and programmed a location into the console computer.

As the car kicked into gear, she turned to us. There was no reason for her to steer or even watch the road. The computer did that for her. What's more, Mia didn't need to break or accelerate because the sensors knew when to do that.

"We're going to drive around the city," she said. "I want you to tell me when you see an other-worlder."

I exchanged a glance with Kitten, who sat on my left.

"Are we being graded on this?" Cara asked.

"With your lives," was the dead-serious answer.

Several girls groaned. My heartbeat sped into hyperdrive.

Mia frowned. "I'm not going to kill you, if that's what you're thinking. In the real world, you have to spot the aliens before they spot you. Don't assume that just because most of them are visually different that you'll be able to know when one is near. They hide. They sneak. Some of them can even transport right in front of you and kill you before you realize what's happened." Her frown deepened. "In my early days as an agent, I was attacked from behind and almost died. Had I been paying attention, I could have killed the alien before he knew I was there."

Silence.

All of us were busy staring out the windows, searching . . . searching . . . for the elusive enemy among us. The enemy who would kill us if we didn't kill him first. I saw only tall syn-oaks that knifed the skyline and thick bushes, freshly planted since there weren't enough trees and the government was always looking for ways to replenish.

To my right, Emma shifted. I'd sat by her on purpose. I needed to apologize to her. I never should have mentioned her trauma. She'd been opening up to me, animated for the first time since I'd met her, and I'd reminded her of what she'd gone through.

Like she'd said, I didn't want people to know about my drug use because they always—okay, usually—treated me differently. Emma probably felt the same. There was shame in knowing that others knew your deep, dark secrets.

I should wait until we were alone, or at the very least wait until this assignment was complete, but . . . screw the assignment. My teammate came first. "I'm sorry," I whispered to her.

She turned away, giving me her back.

"We all have our secrets, Emma," I said in that same quiet tone. "You've heard mine. I was a drug addict. What you don't know is that I've spent six months in rehab before coming to this camp—and that wasn't the first time. It was just the first time I decided to get clean."

At first, I didn't think I'd reached her, but then she slowly pivoted in her seat and faced me. "I used to fly, too," she admitted softly.

My eyes widened. I'd thought I was the only one here with such a stain on her record. "I didn't know."

"I was stupid enough to take Onadyn while swimming and I was coming down from the high when I realized I was surrounded by a group of—" Her voice had begun shaking and she paused. "A group of Lyrosses. They were . . . I was . . ." She stopped again, but this time she didn't start back up.

I reached over and squeezed her hand. She covered my hand with her palm. I could guess how the event came about. When she'd come to, the Outers had already been in the process of raping her. She would have been weak, dehydrated. She wouldn't have been able to fight.

Nothing I said could comfort her, I knew that. But I said, "We're learning how to neutralize creatures like that."

"I will kill them." Hate dripped from her voice. "I will."

"And I'll help."

We shared a smile.

"Girls," Mia said. "What's so important that you're not paying attention as ordered?"

"Teamwork," I said. "A very wise instructor once told me that a good team worked together but a great team liked each other."

Her lips curled into an amused, dry grin. "Good answer, but you'd better start paying attention or I'll whip your asses. We've already passed two Arcadians and no one noticed."

"Well, hell," Kitten muttered. "I was paying attention and I didn't see them."

"They know how to hide, how to blend into the shadows. *Look.*"

I craned my neck until I peered over Emma's shoulder. I didn't release her hand, though, and she didn't release mine. I studied, I observed, I scanned, really I did, but I saw only the occasional tree. The moon was a tiny sliver, muted and thin, not very helpful.

Soon we reached the edge of the city, away from the pier, and there were a few more lights. Lots more buildings. Not many people were out at this hour, but there were a few cars on the road.

Scattered throughout were hookers and druggies in need of a fix. They stumbled around, soliciting anyone who would listen. They were dirty and probably desperate. *That could have been me one day,* I realized. It was humbling. Shaming. But also invigorating. I'd broken the cycle. That *wouldn't* be me.

From the corner of my eye, I saw movement. I shifted and sharpened my gaze into the swell of buildings. Saw nothing. I scanned the area. There! Adrenaline raced through my veins. A stooped body that was hairless and wrinkled bounded from one corner of a building to another.

"Look! A Sybilin," I said, pointing.

Mia's blue eyes widened and she followed the length of my arm. "Where?"

"There."

A second later, she cursed under her breath. "Where there's one, there's a horde." She ordered the car to stop. In the next instant, the tires squealed and we were thrown forward.

"Stay here," Mia said as she withdrew a pyre-gun. "Open," she commanded, and one of the doors instantly obeyed. She jumped outside, yelled, "Close and lock," over her shoulder, and was off.

She disappeared down a dark alleyway. One heartbeat passed. Two. Blue beams erupted, lighting up the night. I thought I heard a scream. Thought I saw a shadow move. Then, nothing.

"I wonder what Jenn's doing now," I said. Wrong topic, I realized a second later. It really brought down everyone's morale. I was happy when Kitten changed the subject.

"I bet Mia nailed him." Grinning, Kitten clapped. "He's probably begging for death."

Everyone glued their noses to the right window, watching and waiting.

"I know one thing," Lindsay said. "I never want to piss that woman off. There's murder in her eyes."

I agreed. Still, I couldn't help but like and admire her. "Think she can beat up her boyfriend?"

Cara barked out a laugh. "Probably. I pity the poor fool. I bet he has to wear iron underwear to protect himself from her anger."

I bit my lip to keep from smiling. "She's not that bad."

"Are you kidding me?" Lindsay's red eyebrows winged into her equally red hairline. "My first day at camp, she knocked me on my ass for no reason."

"Ha!" Cara wagged a finger at her. "Your first day here, you told her that you hoped she liked the taste of tile because you were going to use her face as a mop."

"No, you did *not*," I gasped out.

Emma covered her mouth to hide her grin.

Lindsay's cheeks colored, the exact shade of her hair. "I didn't want to become anyone's bitch, okay," she admitted. "And I'd always heard that the best way to send a message that you shouldn't be messed with was to find the strongest person and knock them down."

"But Mia?" I shook my head and *tsk*ed under my tongue. "That's just asking for a beatdown."

Mia returned a few seconds later and conversation ceased. We jumped back into our seats as she peeked her head inside the car. "Help me load him on top, girls, and then we're heading back." Her tone was grim, chasing away our momentary amusement. "This exercise is officially over. I didn't see his friends, but I know they're out there. We've got to warn Boss."

14

The drive home was quiet and tension-filled.

I wished Jenn had been there; she would have said something to lighten the mood. When we returned—I don't know how Mia found the invisible building—she entered some sort of code on a remote and the shield dropped, leaving a perfect view of the camp. Except there was only a rough-hewn doorway and a hill. That I could see, at least. The rest had to be underground.

She ushered us inside and to the Common. "Get some rest," she said, distracted. "Classes start soon."

Unconcerned with the Sybilins, the girls yawned and trekked off to their rooms. I remained in the doorway, too wired to sleep.

Realizing I wasn't beside her anymore, Kitten glanced over her shoulder and stopped. Her orange, gold, and brown hair had come loose from its band and now tumbled down her back in tangles. "You coming?"

"Not yet. I'm going to work out or something."

"Want company?"

"Nah. Go on."

"Sure?"

I nodded.

"Good, 'cause I'm about to pass out."

We shared a grin and then she was off. The halls were empty as I strode to the gym, ready to expend some unwanted energy. I ID'd in with a hand scan and approached the virtual boxing ring.

Those Sybilins . . . I was worried about them. About the damage they could do to the people of New Chicago. What if one of them got to my mom? What if they killed her? What if—damn it, there were so many "what ifs." The girls didn't know what they could do, they hadn't seen. They hadn't been attacked that night in the forest.

Mia had said there were always others, but she hadn't seen any. Had they seen us, then? Hidden? Or had they followed us? I wasn't ready to face those water suckers again. My skin was still flaking from the last time. Next time I fought them, I wanted to have the expert skill of an A.I.R. agent. I wanted to do major damage.

I wanted to kick ass.

"What are you doing here?"

Gasping at the unexpected interruption, I spun around. Ryan was leaning one shoulder against the wall. Sweat trickled down his temples and neck, as if he'd just worked out. Hardcore. Strands of wet hair were plastered to his head.

He looked fantastic. And he'd spoken to me.

"What are *you* doing here?"

"Honestly?" he said, then frowned. "I have no idea. You?"

"I couldn't sleep," I admitted.

His frown slowly inched into a wry smile. "Me neither, but I bet your sleeplessness is for an entirely different reason."

"Yeah?" I regarded him silently. Something about his words caused my stomach to clench. No, I realized in the next second. Not his words. My stomach clenched at what he *didn't* say. He wanted sex; *that's* why he couldn't sleep. "What's your reason?" I wanted to hear him say it. Dangerous, I know.

He didn't reply for a moment, just looked at me. His ice-blue eyes were filled with heat. A heat I'd seen before—and liked. A heat that did crazy things to my heartbeat and to the blood flowing through my veins. "What, you're ignoring me again? I asked you a question, Stone."

He rolled his eyes. "That's 'Mr. Stone' to you."

I snorted. He was Ryan to me. Not once had I thought of him as Mr. Stone.

Ryan straightened and closed the distance between us. I drew in a deep breath, absorbing the male scent of him. "Well?" I insisted.

He tapped me on the end of the nose and said, "You. You're the reason I can't sleep."

"Oh." The word slipped from me, a breathless sigh. He'd

given me the answer I'd wanted to hear, the answer I'd expected, and a tremble worked through me. I liked this guy, way more than I should. Way more than was wise. And every time I saw him, I only liked him more.

"What's your reason, Miss Germaine?" he asked.

It was hard to think with him in front of me, his hot blue gaze boring into me. I wanted to repeat his answer, but didn't dare. The truth was hazardous to my health. Instead, I sidestepped his question and told him about the tour I'd just taken and how it had been cut short.

His nostrils flared in anger. "Those Sybilins . . . I hate them. They multiply and kill, multiply and kill. Like a virus."

I studied him for a moment. "I'm glad you came that night in the forest. We would have died without you."

"We'd heard they were in the area, but none of us had actually seen one. Then one of Allison's old friends called her and invited her to the party. We came alone because we didn't want to alarm the kids or alert them to our presence, but backup was supposed to have arrived earlier if needed."

Kids. I ran my tongue over my teeth. He'd just lumped me into that "kid" category. I didn't want him to see me as a kid. *It's for the best, Phoenix. You know it is.* "Why didn't they?"

"They were fighting Sybilins somewhere else. The creatures were out in droves that night." Ryan tilted his head toward the boxing ring. "You came to work out, right? Well, let's work you out."

My heart skipped a beat. "Together?"

"Why not?"

I threw my arms in the air. "Because you don't look at me or touch me anymore."

"I'm looking at you right now." And he was. His eyes were still blazing that blue fire, hotter than before.

"Why?" I asked, a sudden catch in my throat. "Why now?"

"Tonight I'm feeling dangerous. Daring."

So was I, I realized. I hadn't been able to admit my feelings, but I did want him to touch me. Very badly. I could tell he was on the verge of changing his mind, though, of the danger he'd admitted was so exciting. He was already stepping backward, away from me.

"You don't look like you're into danger." *Stupid. This is stupid.* "Sure you can take me?" I taunted in a way that was guaranteed to get him inside the ring. Boys couldn't tolerate jabs to their prowess. "Afraid I'll knock you on your ass again?"

He paused and smiled wryly. "I guess we'll find out, won't we?" He latched onto my shoulders, spun me around, and gave my lower back a gentle push. "You've been doing very well in class. You focus. You have strength. Speed. What you don't have is a killer instinct."

"I do, too!" I stepped into the ring marked by red lines on the floor.

Ryan stepped in behind me. "Ring. Lock," he said. Then to me, he said, "No, you don't. You think you have it, but you don't."

The air swirled and solidified over the lines, then

branched upward until we were encased in a clear, solid box. No room to run. Only room to fight and fight some more.

"I'm not going to go easy on you," he said. There was relish in his voice.

"Good. I don't want you to." I'd thought to fight a hologram, but Ryan was better. Much, much better. Cuter, sexier. "And just so you know, I don't plan to go easy on you, either."

"Funny." He didn't give me any warning. In the next flash of time, he leapt forward, grabbed my shoulder, and spun me around, placing us chest to back.

Startled, I didn't react and that failure cost me. Ryan was able to lock his hands around my neck and squeeze. I tried to elbow him, but he expected it and dodged. I tried to step on his foot, but again, he expected it and moved out of my line of fire.

"Back to where we started," he said. "Distract me once, my bad. Distract me twice, I don't think so."

What should I do? What the hell should I do? I could *not* let him beat me so easily. But he was stealing the very breath from my lungs, squeezing harder than he had that first time.

"I'm tough on you because I want you to survive," he said. "I don't want you hurt out there."

Forcing myself to calm, I latched onto his wrists. He squeezed tighter, just hard enough to remind me of Breathless. What he didn't know was that it took more to cut off my airways than it required for most people. Took longer to render me unconscious, too.

Who would have thought there would be a bright side to drug use?

I can do this. I can. I bent down, bringing Ryan with me and letting his weight fall onto my back.

"What are you doing?" he bit out.

Using all of my leg strength, I crouched and bucked up my butt, flinging Ryan over my head. He hit and rolled, forced to let go of me. I wasn't given any time to gloat, though.

"Good thinking," he said, swiping out his arms and knocking my ankles together.

I crashed to my butt, hard. But before I even hit, he was on top of me, his knees at my temples, his, uh, crotch at my throat. As I gasped and struggled, he pinned my shoulders to the ground and gave me the rest of his weight.

"What are you going to do now?" he asked.

Panting, I stared up at him. Damn it! I had tried, but he'd still beat me quickly and easily and the knowledge stung. "Pout," I snapped. "I'm going to pout."

He nearly choked on a laugh. Good. It would save me the trouble of killing him later. "No reason to pout," he said. "All you have to do is work one of your legs between us and kick. Got it?"

I nodded, but didn't attempt it. The longer he stayed where he was, the more I realized I, uh, kind of liked it.

"You did good, Phoenix. Real good."

"No, I didn't," I grumbled. "You're just trying to make me feel better."

"Is it working?"

"No. I can do better than this."

"Really? What could you have done differently?"

"I don't know. Jam my palm into your nose, sending cartilage into your brain. Chop block your throat, crushing your trachea. Knee your balls, making you cough them out."

His eyes sparkled with pride. "Funny."

"True."

"But you did none of those things. And you know why?" His lips twitched as he fought a grin. "No killer instinct. Just. Like. I. Told. You."

Anger rocked me to the bone. No killer instinct. *Grrr.* I'd show him! "You wanna see killer instinct? I'll show you killer instinct."

He released me and stood. He even motioned me over. "Do it, then. I dare you."

I stood to shaky legs, and we faced off. "Sure you're ready for this?"

"Come and get me, sweetheart. I'm ready for whatever you've got to give, sweetheart."

I didn't leap into action, but circled him. As I walked I lost the heat of my anger. I lost my "killer instinct." Not that I'd ever had one. Not with Ryan. We both knew I'd been blowing smoke. I just wanted him. Only him. I wanted him back on top of me, kissing me. Finally.

He watched me, followed my every move with his heated gaze. "That's it? That's all you've got?"

"Maybe."

His brows winged into his hairline. "What are you waiting for? Attack," he commanded.

I almost grinned. "I'm stalking."

He barked out another laugh and threw his arms in the air. "Stalking like this won't scare your enemy."

I might want him, and I might have lost my instinct, but I didn't hesitate. While he was distracted, I attacked. I spun, using my speed and momentum to kick. My foot connected with his stomach. Gasping, he bent over. I rushed him, slamming my elbow into the top of his head.

Crack.

He fell to his face. And he didn't move. I'd hit him harder than I'd meant to. But he should have been able to handle it. Right? Surely. He had to be playing. Eyes narrowed, I kicked him in the side.

He didn't make a nosie.

My heart drummed erratically in my chest. Oh God. Oh no. "Ryan?"

No response.

"Ryan?"

Still nothing.

Ohmygod! What had I done? "Ryan, I'm sorry. So sorry." I bent down and gently clasped his shoulder, meaning to ease him to his back. Before I could blink, he had a vise grip on my wrist and flipped me to my back. "What the—" I hit and he rolled on top of me, squishing the breath from my lungs.

Once again, I was pinned.

"Told you," he said, grinning. "No killer instinct. And that's like the oldest trick ever."

"You dirty little—"

"Uh, uh, uh." He *tsk*ed under his tongue. "You lost. Twice. Accept it."

"Hell no. You cheated."

"Whether you lose by trickery or not, you still lose. Fighting dirty is more than okay, it's expected. Haven't I taught you that?"

I gnashed my molars together. "I *was* winning."

"*Was* doesn't matter. Only the end matters." His face inched closer to mine. So close. "How do you get out of this position?"

"Try to knee you in the balls?"

He laughed. "No. That would cause me to double over, closer to you, and I'd still be able to hit you. You'd work your knees up and kick me in the stomach, like I told you before."

"Maybe later," I whispered. I could feel his breath on my nose. I could feel him all over, in fact. And I liked it. I bit my bottom lip. I liked it a lot.

He lost all trace of amusement, and his eyes darkened hungrily. His breathing became choppy. He knew what I was thinking because he was obviously thinking it, too. "This is stupid," he said.

"Yes."

"This is wrong."

"Yes." But why did it feel so right?

"Do you care?"

I didn't hesitate. "Not right now."

I'd barely gotten the words out before he was kissing me. His tongue swept into my open, waiting mouth and his taste consumed my thoughts. Decadent. Exquisite. Wonderful. Better than anything I could have imagined.

His hands tangled in my hair, and he angled my face for deeper contact. His lips were soft, hungry, and he fed me pure passion. Something I'd never really experienced before.

"I want you," he panted.

"Yes." Yes, yes, yes.

If he stopped kissing me, I'd . . . I'd . . . I don't know. I wound my hands around him, anchoring one at the base of his neck, one at his waist, holding him captive. I lifted up and thrust my tongue back into his mouth.

He moaned. I groaned.

Delicious.

Of course I'd been kissed before, but all those times faded from my mind. There was only here, now, and Ryan. He was strength, and he was fire. He was *everything* just then. I felt inexperienced. I felt vulnerable.

"Phoenix," he breathed, like a prayer.

"Ryan."

Slowly he pulled away from me. "If I don't stop now, I won't be able to." Tension layered his voice.

"Then don't stop," I said, staring up at him. "Just a little more."

"A little more," he agreed. Leaning down, he kissed me a second time. This kiss was hotter, more dangerous. His hands roved the length of my body, stopping at my breasts and kneading. My nipples hardened.

He tore away from me yet again. He was panting as he crouched on his knees. I lay where I was, needy, achy.

"I've never done anything like this before," he said darkly. "I've been an instructor for over a year and I've never wanted a student. I never even dated another trainee."

"Ryan," I said. *Kiss me.*

He scrubbed a hand down his face. "We'll be punished for that. Boss will know. He always knows." Ryan stood. He didn't speak a word as he disabled the ring and strode away from me.

"Ryan," I called.

He stopped at the doorway. I don't know what I planned to say, but neither of us were given a chance to find out. An alarm suddenly erupted throughout the room, its shrill warning sending chills through my spine.

Ryan spun around and faced me. "Shit. *Shit.*"

"What's going on?" Fear coursed through me. Was the alarm for *us*? For our kiss?

"We've been invaded."

15

"This is not a drill," the computerized voice said over the intercom. "Repeat, this is not a drill."

I jumped to my feet. Ryan was already racing back to me. He grabbed my wrist and tugged me forward. "Come on."

Confusion rocked me. "I don't understand what's happening."

"We're being attacked, Phoenix. This has only happened once before, years ago, but half of the student body was killed." He had to speak loudly to be heard over the alarm. "If a sector is breeched, the computer usually locks all doorways, preventing the invader from moving from room to room. But the alarms are screeching and I haven't heard the locks click. That means part of the system has been compromised."

"And *that* means . . ."

"Everyone is fair game," he said bleakly. "Now come on."

He raced to the far wall and splayed his hands in a section that looked like every other section.

Blue lights scanned him from head to toe, and the wall opened into an arsenal. Tier after tier displayed guns, knives, throwing stars, and weapons I didn't recognize. My jaw nearly hit the ground. "That's . . . that's . . ."

"Plan B. There's an arsenal in every room of the building," Ryan said. "Including your room. You're just not in the database to open the locks."

Wow. I'd never known, never suspected. Maybe that was a good thing. "How could anyone know about this place and attack it? It's invisible."

"I don't know how they did it, but we'll worry about that later."

"Sybilins have bypassed security," the computer said. "There are four Sybilins in sectors one, two, and three."

Sybilins? My fear intensified, branching to every part of my body.

"Shit. It's worse than I thought." Ryan sheathed several knives at his waist and palmed a pyre-gun. He tossed it at me, and I deftly caught it. "Hope you learned how to use one of those."

I gulped. "I've practiced, and I almost always hit what I aim at."

"Almost is better than never. The gun is locked on stun right now, so you don't have to worry about killing anyone. But don't fire if your friends or an instructor is nearby. If any of them carry alien blood, they'll be frozen in place and helpless."

"Only Kitten is alien, and I swear to God I won't aim in her direction."

Ryan snorted. "She's not the only one, Phoenix."

My eyes widened. "What?"

"Siren. Angel." Pause. "Boss."

"What? But they look . . . they look . . . completely human. And your dad? That would mean . . ."

"Yeah. Who better to track aliens than aliens? Does this change your opinion of me?" he asked with the slightest trace of bitterness.

"No." It didn't. Not at all. I was just shocked. "Does the government know?"

"Of course. There are a select few who are trusted, but that's something the general public can never know. And something you might never have been taught." Another pause. "If you don't want to engage the Sybilins, if you don't think you are ready to handle this, lock yourself in your room. Better yet, just reactivate the boxing ring." He faced me as he said it, eyes staring deeply. Probing. "The Outers won't know how to bypass it, I hope, and you'll be safe."

Hide away like a coward? Hide away while others fought—and maybe died. *I'd* rather die. I was here to become an agent, so I would damn well act like one. No matter how scared I was.

"I'm ready," I said, straightening my back.

"Good," Ryan said, but he didn't look happy about it. He looked mad and proud and scared. Yes, scared. For me? "Stay safe, Phoenix. Promise me."

"I promise."

He kissed me. No tongue this time, but a swift meshing of lips. Hard, comforting, giving. "Let's do this."

He rushed out of the gym, and I stayed close on his heels. Chaos awaited us in the halls. Agents rushed in every direction, laden down with weapons. Students raced, too, but they were panicked, their wild gazes scanning as they demanded to know what was going on.

"Three Sybilins have breeched sector four," the computer said. Pause. "Five Sybilins have breeched sector five."

From the end of the hall, Kitten spotted me and sprinted to my side. Her face was pale, and her lips were pulled tight with worry. "I was sleeping and all of a sudden the alarms were going off and I nearly jumped out of my skin and I don't have any clue about what's going on and—"

I grabbed her arm to silence the babbling. "We're under attack. Sybilins like to fuse their lips with their prey and suck the water out of their bodies. Whatever you do, do not let one get on top of you. Understand?"

Her skin became even more pallid, but her pupils elongated like they did before she engaged in battle. Determination squared her shoulders. "I— Yes. I understand."

I jumped back into motion, dragging her with me and

closing in on Ryan. "Use any weapons you can find," I said to Kitten. "Wait, I'll get you one." Reaching out, I withdrew one of the knives from Ryan's waist. He almost sliced my arm off, but caught himself when he realized it was me. Note to self: Never take a weapon from Ryan without asking. I slapped the hilt into Kitten's palm. "Tell the others, okay. Warn them."

"I will." She turned to the wall. My brow furrowed in confusion. What was she— Dear God. She'd just disappeared through it! She'd actually walked through the wall; there one moment, gone the next.

My (kind of) boyfriend was half alien, and my best friend had superpowers.

I wanted to marvel at that, but didn't have time. Ryan and I hauled butt into the Common. There, we spied several Sybilins. They were crawling all over the walls. Like insects. The door to the agent's section was open, and I could see Bradley, Erik, and a few others trying to get to the girls' area to protect them, I was sure, as a true agent would do. But the Sybilins spotted them and attacked, knocking them down.

Erik fought his way out in a bid to get to Bradley.

Before my eyes, one of the creatures lowered its head . . . touched its lips to Bradley's . . .

"No!" I shouted. Not again. My friends would not be hurt. Bradley began jerking.

Ryan cursed. I screamed, filled with more rage than ever before. *These creatures will not hurt my friends again,* my mind repeated over and over. At least I knew what to do this time.

I aimed the pyre-gun and fired, just as Ryan did the same. Blue beams erupted from mine, red from Ryan's. The Sybilin on top of Bradley froze at the same moment a hole was burned into his back, and Bradley was able to kick the thing off himself.

"It . . . it . . ." Bradley's voice was shaky, and he grasped at his throat.

Ryan fired another round, hitting a Sybilin behind Bradley.

Ryan wasn't using stun, I realized. The red-gold blast was frying everything it touched. He fired again, and this round slammed into the creature trying to subdue Erik, burning the skin from its bones. Erik shouted and scrambled away from the screaming inferno. His eyebrows were singed.

As I stunned as many water-sucking monsters as I could, Angel pounded into the Common. I almost paused and gaped at her. Almost. I'd never seen her so . . . enraged. Her eyes glowed with an unholy fire of their own, and her body moved as if it were pure electricity, flitting from one wire to another.

She was a frightening sight to behold.

"Not everyone is human," Ryan had said. Yeah, I believed him. Angel didn't look human just then. Which species was she? Whatever it was, she was spellbinding, mesmerizing. Beautiful. She clutched two knives, each with a pronged, serrated edge, and she used them with abandon. The Sybilins' yellow, puss-filled blood splattered as she moved and killed as if it were a dance.

Mia Snow pounded in behind her, just as lethal. "Bastards," she snarled, punching anything stupid enough to get near her. "Die!" Her gaze caught mine and she worked her way toward me.

"What should I do?"

"Keep freezing them. They set us up," she growled, never slowing. "I didn't think they were smart enough to do it, but they followed us here. They attacked tonight so I wouldn't have time to question the one I stunned. Behind you!"

I whipped around—and saw a creature bounding toward me. Le'Ace jumped in my path and cut its throat. Thick yellow blood dripped from her hands. There was no expression on her face. I understood now why they were so hard on us, why they made us obey without hesitation and punished us if we didn't. Why they took our freedom and constantly wanted us at our very best.

Everything they did was meant to save our lives.

"Twelve Sybilins have breached sector six," the computer said.

The room was suddenly flooded with more of them. The creatures hopped everywhere in their frenzy to get to us. I aimed and fired, aimed and fired, freezing as many as I could.

Ryan worked beside me, never leaving my side. We made a good team. But my gun eventually gave out, forcing me to use another weapon: my hands. The Sybilins were salivating, eager for more water.

Siren strutted into the room as if she hadn't a care in the

world. She hummed under her breath. The Sybilians paused, pointed ears perching as they listened to her. Distracted as they were, I launched forward and kicked one in the middle. Contact. It howled. Another pulled itself from Siren's spell and came at my right. I spun, ducked, and punched. Two more appeared at my other side. I crouched low, spinning my leg as I'd been taught by Ryan and knocked the creatures together.

"Phoenix! Catch."

I turned at the sound of my name. Ryan tossed me a blade, and I caught the hilt. My heart pounded frantically in my chest. I could see another Sybilin coming toward me . . . in the air . . . about to land on top of me . . .

I stabbed without thought. Kill, yes, I could kill. I *would* kill. I had killed, and I felt no guilt. Some people might call me a murderer, but I was an agent. I was doing my job, my duty.

The metal sunk into its belly. Yellow blood, warm and thick, oozed over my hands. I tried not to gag. It smelled bad, like rotten garbage. *Keep fighting. I have to take out as many as I can.*

Panting, I looked for my next opponent. Still the war raged.

I threw myself into a group trying to latch onto Cara. Erik was there, cursing as he fought to save her. He moved with lithe grace and potent fury. Sweat trickled from my temples as I stabbed, turned, stabbed, soaking my hair to my head. My muscles burned; my arms shook.

I didn't slow. I couldn't.

Four of the creatures jumped onto Ryan, subduing him with their sheer numbers. In that moment, I went a little crazy. My strength intensified, riding the waves of an already intense adrenaline rush. The other agents were fully engaged and didn't realize that Sybilins were fusing their mouths onto any part of Ryan's body they could reach, sucking his energy, sucking away his life.

Dimly, I thought I heard Allison Stone shout. Thought I heard Kitten hiss. Then Emma was at my side, rushing to Ryan, as well. We reached him at the same time, and she grabbed one of the Sybilins by the neck and ripped it off Ryan.

She punched the creature in the face.

I think she saw the Lyrosses in these Sybilins, because there was death in her eyes, a need to kill in her expression. Once she started punching, she didn't stop.

I elbowed and kicked two of the monsters, cutting them as I did so, ensuring they wouldn't get back up. Finally, there was only one left. Its lips were attached to Ryan's. Ryan's struggles were weakening, and I could see the dryness of his skin, the vagueness of his eyes. His body spasmed.

"You want to get wet," I spat at the creature. "Then I'll get you wet." I slashed out, but the Sybilin moved and I only managed to graze its shoulder.

Thankfully, though, it released Ryan and bounced on top of me, trying to lower its lips. I saw its glowing eyes, red, hungry. One of its hands wrapped around my wrists, preventing me from using the knife. I flailed, trying to dislodge it.

I'd been in this position before, with Ryan. *Don't panic,* I thought. *Remember what he told you to do.* His words echoing in my mind, I worked up one of my legs, until it was between me and the Sybilin. I kicked with every ounce of energy I possessed. The alien sailed backward. I didn't allow myself a moment's rest but jumped forward, gripping my knife, and cut.

It howled, then dropped to the floor, immobile.

I stood in place, gasping. Ryan looked up at me, his features pained.

"Thank you," he managed. "Thank you."

"My pleasure." I was just about to jump back into the fight when another Sybilin fell at my feet. I blinked in surprise.

"It's over," Mia said, panting. "They're dead."

"Enemy neutralized," the computer said, confirming Mia's words.

Suddenly weary, I gazed around. Shock, yes. Pride, that too. But most of all, I experienced sadness. Yellow rivers branched from the bodies lying on the floor. Not all of them were Sybilins, though. My stomach clenched, and I prayed to God I didn't find one of my friends dead.

Ryan eased to a sitting position, weak but okay. I looked past him . . . and that's when I saw Kitten. She was unmoving.

Panicked, I stumbled to her and knelt down. "Kitten?" I shook her shoulder. "Kitten!"

Her eyelids fluttered open weakly. "What?"

"Thank God." I sighed in relief. "Are you hurt?"

"Only my pride," she said dryly. "One of those bastards knocked me down and tried to kiss me, but I remembered what you said and scratched its eyes out." A dark cloud blanketed her expression as her gaze scanned the room. "Is Bradley okay?"

"I'm right here," he said, bending over her. His freckles appeared black against his too-pale skin. "You okay?"

"I'm good," she grumbled, but she smiled up at him. "Did we win or what?"

"Oh, yes," I said. "We won."

16

In the following days, the buildings were cleaned and the injured doctored. Both Kitten and Ryan spent two days on an IV. I visited them as often as I was allowed. There was always another agent in Ryan's room, though, so I never got a chance to talk to him about the kiss. And I wanted to talk to him. Badly.

One of those days I was summoned to Angel's office. She didn't say a word as she blindfolded me and drove me away from the school. Sweat beaded over my skin. My nails bit into my palms. I expected my memory to be wiped for daring to break a rule and kiss an instructor (and wanting to do it again), but she merely escorted me . . . somewhere and sat me down at the only piece of furniture in the room. A table.

She removed the hood, and I blinked against the sudden light. "Where am I?" I asked nervously.

"An abandoned warehouse we like to use."

"For what?" I gulped past the lump in my throat.

Angel hooked a lock of light brown hair behind her ear, her expression unreadable. "You'll see."

"I thought I got three strikes, not two. I thought—" My mother entered, and my mouth formed a large O. "Mom?"

"Phoenix." She hesitated in the doorway, then tilted her chin with determination and marched forward. "How are you?"

Angel stepped away from the table, giving us a sense of privacy without actually giving us privacy.

I pushed to my feet. I couldn't believe this. It was more surreal than having Outers attack the camp.

"How are you?" my mom repeated. Her familiar brown eyes swept over me. "You look well."

"I am," I said shakily. "You?"

"I'm good." She chewed on her bottom lip. "They tell me you're doing well. That they test you every day and you're clean."

"I am."

"I— I'm proud of you." Her features crumpled, followed quickly by her shoulders. She stared down at her hands.

Had she just said . . . surely she hadn't . . .

"I am. I'm proud of you. I let you go without saying good-bye, and I've hated myself ever since. I just—"

With those words, I experienced a tide of relief. Of joy. Of happiness. I rushed to her and wrapped her in my arms. "It's okay. Really. Sending me to camp was the best thing that could have ever happened to me. I'm clean. I've made great friends, and I finally have a purpose."

"That's all I've ever wanted for you." She squeezed me tightly. "I love you."

"And I love you."

Angel piped in and said, "We need to get back, Ms. Germaine. I'm sorry."

My mom scrubbed her watery eyes with the back of her wrist, and gave Angel a half smile. "I understand."

I hugged her again. "Write me."

"I will. I miss you."

"I miss you, too."

This time, we said good-bye. I smiled the entire drive to camp, joy bubbling from me. My mother loved me. She was proud of me. Life had never been better.

The next day, all of the students were called together. We'd partied here before, but now we were going to celebrate our victory. There were decorations and streamers, a colorful, festive river. Music played in the background. I stood off to the side, watching the dancing.

Kitten looked completely healed and was locked in a tight embrace with Bradley, not caring who saw them. Cara danced with Erik, and there was worship in his eyes. I experienced a pang of envy. I wanted that with Ryan. And I knew I couldn't have it.

Speaking of Ryan, where was he? He was out of the hospital, I knew that much. I wanted to see him. *Needed* to see him.

Just then, Boss entered the room. Conversations tapered to quiet, and the music died down. Ryan was beside him as if my thoughts had summoned him. My heart hammered against my ribs and my gaze drank him up. His gaze did the same to me. The rest of the instructors, including Allison, Mia, Angel, and Siren, entered, as well, and lined up behind him.

Boss spoke, his voice echoing throughout the room as if he wore a mic. "I want to commend each and every one of you for your bravery. You handled yourselves like true agents. I'm proud. Very proud."

Everyone cheered.

He allowed it to continue for several minutes, then held up his hand for silence. "You were given a glimpse of just how evil some aliens can be. I hope this strengthens your resolve to become the best agent you can be."

Kitten, Emma, and the rest of our gang inched beside me, and they were nodding. Hell, even I nodded. I wanted to be a good agent. The best. I wanted to protect my world. My friends. My mother.

"There are far worse out there," Boss continued. "But as for today, we aren't going to worry about them. Now that everyone is healed and out of medical, we're going to celebrate. Dance. Eat. Laugh. Classes are dismissed for the rest of the afternoon. Tomorrow, however, we'll continue on schedule."

Cheers abounded once more. Clapping. Whistling. Once by one, the instructors filed out of the room. My gaze bore into Ryan's back until the last possible second. The music kicked up again and kids started dancing, arms flying, bodies flailing. Bradley and Erik high-fived before Bradley pulled Kitten back onto the dance floor. Erik grabbed Cara and followed suit.

A tall, handsome boy approached Emma and asked her to dance. She glanced at me with uncertainty, and I nodded encouragingly. Her cheeks reddened, but she nodded. The boy grinned, and the two of them were off.

Alone, I sighed.

Not knowing my punishment for kissing Ryan was the only black spot in my life. *Well, I can fix that.* Yeah, I could. Right now. Knowing what I had to do, I raced after Boss, spying him and the others in the hallway. "Boss," I called.

All of the instructors turned toward me, confused. Boss stopped, faced me, and dismissed the others with a wave of his hand. Everyone but Ryan. He latched onto Ryan's wrist, holding him in place.

"Now is as good a time as any," he said. "My office. Both of you." He was wearing his dark glasses, so I couldn't read his expression. His voice, though, was harsh.

My heart began pounding in my chest as I followed behind him, through restricted area after restricted area and into his office. Ryan didn't look at me. His back was stiff, his hands clenched into fists.

Ryan took a position in front of the desk. I came up beside him as Boss claimed the chair in front. The multiple screens behind him were blank.

Ryan didn't deserve to be kicked out just because we'd kissed, but neither did I. We'd done a good job with the Sybilins. *That* should matter more than a little rule breaking. In my opinion, at least.

"Is there something you two want to tell me?" Boss leaned back and anchored his hands over his middle.

"I kissed her," Ryan said at the same time I said, "I kissed him."

We shared an exasperated look. *Shut up,* he mouthed.

You shut up, I returned.

"Both of you shut up," Boss said. "You knew better than to do such a thing. Didn't you?"

Silence.

"Didn't you?" he barked.

"Yes," we said in unison.

He worked his jaw. "How do you think you should be punished then?"

Ryan slapped a hand against the desktop. "Phoenix is not to be blamed. I'm older, and I knew better."

"Ryan is not to be blamed, sir. Only me. I— I forced him!"

Ryan choked, and Boss sighed.

"Kick me out if you feel you must," I added, "but know that you'll be losing a damn good agent."

"Yes, I saw what you did, how you fought. For a student who has been here less than a month, your abilities continue to amaze me. I haven't seen fighting like that since Le'Ace and Mia."

Pride filled me, overshadowing my fear. "Thank you."

He sighed again, loud and long. "This is strike two for you, Phoenix. Ryan, strike one. Don't let it happen again. Do you understand me? Our rules are in effect for a reason."

I swallowed against my relief, my depression, and my panic. Relief because I wasn't being kicked out. Depression because I could not kiss Ryan again. And panic because I had one more chance. Only one. If I messed up, I'd lose everything I'd come to love.

"Get out of here. And tell everyone you were whipped or something. Otherwise I'll have a revolt. God, I'm soft."

Without another word, I turned on my heel and strode from the room, right behind Ryan. When we were alone in the hall, he said, "I'll walk you to the Common."

"All right." We stalked forward. I was trembling. With happiness, with dread. I had so much I wanted to say to him, but the words were suddenly frozen in my throat. He was Ryan, my Ryan, and I had to stay away from him. I couldn't be kicked out.

"I'm proud of you," he said. "You saved me."

Finally I found my voice. "We're even, then, because you saved me that night in the forest."

"You're going to be the best agent this academy has ever produced and . . ." He pushed out a sigh. "I'm sorry I put that in jeopardy."

"I wanted you to kiss me, Ryan." *I still do.* God. An entire year without kissing him. Would I survive? I'd have to, because this program had to be priority one. At least for now. So there could be no more strikes.

A moment passed in silence, and then Ryan did the most amazing thing. He grabbed my wrist and pulled me into a shadowed corner. "What's going on?" I gasped out.

"I set the cameras to turn off sixty seconds after we left the office." He grinned down at me. "We've got two minutes. Let's make the most of it." His lips meshed over mine, his tongue immediately thrusting inside.

I didn't hesitate. My arms twined around his neck, pulling him as close as I could get him. If this kiss had to last us a year, I *was* going to make the most of it. I rubbed myself all over him, trying to sink past his skin. Trying to brand myself with him.

His hands tangled in my hair, and he moaned. My blood was burning, raging through my veins. The kiss became so fervent, our teeth banged together. He even palmed my breast. I leaned deeper into him, silently begging for more.

"Ryan," I urged. "More."

"Phoenix," he moaned. He tongued me deep, so wonderfully deep.

I sucked him with everything I had, memorizing, taking

his breath and giving him mine. But all too soon, he jerked away from me. I groaned at the loss of him.

He was panting, I was panting. With shaky hands, he righted his clothing and helped me right mine. "Time's almost up."

We stood back in the hallway as if we'd never stepped in the corner. We kicked into motion and rounded that very corner. The Common door came into view. I could hear voices beyond it, happy voices. Laughing voices.

At the door, Ryan stopped. I stopped. This was it. The end of the road. Ryan didn't move or speak for several seconds. Then, he folded me in a hug, whispering, "We'll find a way to make this work, Phoenix, even if we have to wait until you graduate."

"Yes," I whispered back. *Yes, yes, yes.* I'd wait for him. He was so worth it. And that he was willing to wait for me . . . God, life was good.

He opened the door for me, and I practically skipped past him. I felt his fingertips close around the ends of my hair, caressing, and then he was moving away from me. I expelled a breath, watching until the door closed and he disappeared.

"Phoenix," I heard Emma call.

I turned, unable to hold back my grin.

She sat on the couch and motioned me over. I joined her, thinking that all suddenly felt right in my life. My mom loved me, Ryan wanted me, I had friends, I wasn't being kicked out of school, and I was turning out to be a great fighter. More than that, I hadn't broken down and used again, even under the most stressful of situations. While battling those Sybilins, drugs had been the last thing on my mind.

"Why'd you leave the party?" I asked her.

"I was looking for you. I wanted to make sure you were okay. Boss was pissed at you."

"I'm better than okay," I said, my grin widening. What a difference from when I first arrived at camp. Truly, I was happier than I'd ever been.

Look out world!

I mean, soon I'd be an agent. A real agent. I'd patrol the streets, keeping Outers from hurting humans. "Come on." Laughing with joy, I dragged Emma back to the celebration and danced the rest of the day away.

Like Boss had said, I was going to enjoy today to its fullest. Tomorrow was another day.

I could hardly wait to face it.

Epilogue

A year later, I found myself—at long freaking last—in bed with Ryan. We'd just spent the most amazing hour doing things we'd only been able to dream about for twelve months. I was sweaty, panting, and grinning. I was more satisfied than I'd ever been in my life.

And yeah, he'd been able to give me an orgasm.

"Happy graduation," he said, snuggling me close.

"That was, without a doubt, the best present. Ever."

He uttered a warm chuckle. "I'll probably congratulate you a few more times today."

"I'd be pissed if you didn't. I mean, Mia asked me and the girls to join the New Chicago A.I.R. That deserves another congratulation for sure."

"Yes, it does." His fingers traced over my arm, reminding me of the time I'd seen Erik cuddling Cara, and he kissed my temple. "Your mom okay with that? The job, I mean."

"Yeah." I'd finally told her about the camp, what I'd learned and what I planned to do with my life. She'd been upset at first, but had slowly come to realize that having a purpose was what kept me clean.

"I've been asked to join A.I.R. every year, but remained at the school instead," Ryan said. "Maybe I'll finally take them up on the offer."

"Then *I* can congratulate *you*."

"God, I hope you do."

I rolled to my stomach, peering down at his rumpled hair and satisfied expression. "Think Kitten and Bradley are as happy as we are right now?"

"Who knows?" He tweaked my nose. "They've broken up and gotten back together so many times I can't keep up."

"That's better than Cara and Erik." They'd broken up for good. Erik had graduated a few months before me, and a few months into his time with A.I.R., he'd been caught with Onadyn, found guilty of selling it, and had been arrested, not to mention kicked off the force.

He'd disappeared before anyone had been able to get answers from him, like who his supplier was and how he'd gotten them on the street undetected. Which was why Mia had asked me to hunt him down.

He was to be my first case.

I knew him, and I knew how dealers and users operated. I was the best choice for this mission, she'd told me. I wouldn't let her down.

I was going to find him using all the skills I'd acquired. We were hunter and prey now, no longer friends. We couldn't be. I'd do my job. *And when I catch him, Ryan can congratulate me again,* I thought with a grin.

Let the games begin.

Turn the page for a sneak peek of

BLACKLISTED

by Gena Showalter!

Prologue

Erik Trinity had a system for buying drugs.

Always during the day. Fewer Alien Investigation and Removal agents prowling the streets.

Always in the open. Less chance of being pinned in.

And always in a crowd. Even A.I.R. avoided firing when innocents were around.

He knew this because *he* was an agent. Erik winced, hating himself. How he wished the drugs were part of an undercover assignment. But they weren't. What he did was illegal.

If anyone learned of his extracurricular activities, he would spend the rest of his life in prison. But he refused to stop. He *couldn't* stop.

Too many people relied on him.

Each transaction usually took less than two seconds. He walked one direction and the seller walked in the other. As they passed, they made their switch. Cash for Onadyn. Neither slowed, neither said a word. Just boom. Done.

Today had been no different. He already had several vials in his jacket pocket. His part wasn't over, though. Now it was time to pass them to their new owners.

After checking for a tail and finding nothing suspicious in the laughing throng of people milling about and shopping in New Chicago's pulsing town square, he hopped a bus to the Southern District, the poor side of town. Soon polished chrome-and-glass buildings gave way to crumbling, charred red brick that hadn't seen much repair since the Human-Alien War some seventy years ago.

The streets became less crowded, and the people who occupied them less . . . clean. Both humans and Outers resided here, but Erik mainly saw Outers slumped against dilapidated walls—white-haired Arcadians, six-armed Delenseans, catlike Terans—either too sick or too weak to move.

Judging by a few frozen expressions, some were probably already dead. Erik's hands clenched at his sides. What senseless deaths. Preventable and unnecessarily cruel. They so easily could have been saved.

Scowling, he exited at his stop. Warm sunlight instantly washed over him, attracted to the black jacket, T?-?shirt, and jeans he wore. Inconspicuous and forgettable clothing no matter who stood around him.

He performed another perimeter check. Still nothing suspicious. *So close to being done,* he thought, his relief so potent it overshadowed his disgust. He was always on edge until the last vial was out of his possession.

Get it done. Erik kicked into motion along the urine-scented sidewalk, hands in his pockets, head slightly down. He rounded a corner and heard a pain-filled moan. *Don't stop. Don't look.* Yet his gaze zeroed in on a young girl writhing in pain.

Keep moving, one part of him said. He'd seen hundreds of aliens die like this; he'd probably see a hundred more.

Help her, the other part screamed.

He had about an hour, tops, to get the Onadyn to its new owners and catch a ride home. Otherwise, his girlfriend would wake up alone and wonder where he was. And if Cara wondered, Cara would ask questions. She was an agent, too, so she knew how to suck every little scrap of information from him—information that would destroy him.

No, he didn't have time for this. He crouched down anyway.

"Where are your parents?" he gently asked the girl.

"Dead," she managed to rasp out. Her little body jerked, the muscles spasming erratically. Her eyelids squeezed together, cutting off his view of glassy violet eyes. She rolled into a ball.

Dirt smudged her from head to toe, and he could see lice jumping in her snow-white hair. She was Arcadian, probably no more than eight years old. Agony radiated from her. More than most adults could have handled. More than *he* could have handled

"There's no one else to take care of you?" he asked, already sensing the answer.

Her mouth floundered open and closed, but no sound emerged. She was struggling to breathe, no longer able to draw a single molecule of air into her lungs. His stomach knotted as her skin colored blue.

He didn't have an ounce of Onadyn to spare, but he couldn't leave her like this. Without the drug, which allowed certain alien species to tolerate Earth's environment, she would die exactly as the people around her had died. And if that happened, her angel face would haunt him for the rest of his life.

Damn this and damn me. He looked left, then right. No one seemed to be paying them the slightest bit of attention, so he withdrew a clear vial from his pocket. He held it to her lips and poured at least a week's salary down her throat.

He would have to buy more. Which meant lying to Cara (again) and spending money he no longer had (again).

Was it worth it?

Almost instantly, the girl's color began to return, pale cream chasing away pallid blue. Her features smoothed and her body relaxed. A contented smile slowly curled the corners of her lips.

Erik sighed. Yeah, it was worth it. Knowing she would live—at least for a little while—he pushed to his feet and walked away. He didn't look back. For once he felt like the agent he was supposed to be, rather than the despicable agent he'd become.

1

____

A few months later . . .

Have you ever stumbled upon a secret you wished to God
you'd never learned? A dark and dangerous secret? A secret
people would kill to protect?

I have.

And, yeah, I almost died for it.

My name is Camille Robins. I'm eighteen and in my last
month at New Chicago High, District Eight.

It all began on a balmy Friday evening when my friend
Shanel Stacy borrowed her parents' car and picked me up . . .

"I can't believe we're doing this," I said, already breathless
with anticipation and nerves. I slid into the passenger seat.

"Believe it, baby," Shanel said as she buckled into the
driver's side. With a few clicks of the keyboard, she pro-

grammed the Ship's address into the car's console, and we eased out of my driveway and onto the street.

Because sensors kept the car from hitting anyone or thing and because computers navigated the roads, we didn't have to steer or even keep our eyes on our surroundings. We could chat and consider all the things that might go wrong at the famous nightclub.

Get caught lying to our parents—a possibility. We'd told them we were staying the night with another friend of ours. A friend we'd invented. Get thrown out—another possibility. We weren't rich or fabulous like the usual patrons. Make fools of ourselves—the biggest possibility of all.

Neither one of us had style.

Shanel studied me, her intent gaze starting at my dark hair and stopping on my boots. Underneath, my toenails were painted blue to match my eyes. "Why do you look like you're one second away from barfing on the floorboards?"

"I'm not good at clandestine activities. You know that."

"This isn't clandestine. This is *fun*."

"Fun?" So not the word I would have used.

"Oh yeah." Shanel smiled slowly. "Fun." But a moment passed in silence and she lost her grin. Her expression became pensive. "I wish I was an Outer."

Outer. Aka alien. My face scrunched in confusion. "Why?"

"Think about it. Some of them can control humans with their minds. I could make boys fall in love with us; I could force people to notice us; we could become *the* most popular girls at school—no, the world—with only a thought."

Sounded good in theory, but . . . I have nothing against Outers, I just don't want to be one, no matter what their powers are. They lived and walked among us, but some people still hated them and treated them as less than, well, human. I've seen them teased and taunted unmercifully. I've seen them pushed and beaten.

I wanted to be noticed, but I wanted it to be for something good.

Besides, Outers didn't look like us. Some of them had horns. Horns! And not just on their heads. Some of them had blue skin and multiple arms (ick), some of them excreted a gooey green slime (gag). Some of them changed color with their moods (okay, that wasn't so bad).

"What if those mind-controlling powers you want so badly came with a price? Like green scales and fish breath?" I asked. Yeah, some of them had those, too. "Would you still want to be an Outer?"

Shanel shuddered.

I'd take that as a no. Shanel and I were "Invisibles," not seen or heard by our school's elite, but even our socially nonexistent lives were better than those of the Outers. "So, uh, do you think he'll be there?"

She didn't have to ask who *he* was. Erik Troy. Gorgeous,

delectable, mouthwatering Erik Troy. A boy who rarely glanced in my direction, despite the fact that staring at him had become my favorite hobby.

"I told you," Shanel said. "I was standing at my locker and heard Silver tell him they'd meet at the club."

Silver and Erik were best friends and the hottest boys at our school. While Erik was human, Silver was an Outer. A Morevv, one of the most beautiful races I'd ever encountered. I admit it: I wouldn't mind looking like a Morevv, with creamy skin and angelic facial features.

Truly, Silver was the only fully accepted alien I knew.

Shanel wanted him; I wanted Erik (obviously). A perfect match-up for sure: best friends hooking up with best friends. If only the boys would cooperate.

"Think Ivy will be there?" Shanel asked with a bitter edge.

"Probably not." Silver had an on-again-off-again thing with popular Ivy Lynn, a human and someone I'd always wanted to be. The two were currently *off*.

Erik, too, was a free man. But he liked his girls older—or so I'd heard. Probably because *he* looked older than the average high school boy. He was bigger, stronger, more masculine.

"Do I look okay?" I asked, my nervousness increasing.

Shanel's green gaze swept over me and she grinned. "You're like a sexy beast ready to be unleashed."

I couldn't help but return her grin. She'd always had a flare for the dramatic. "Yeah, but do I look *old*?"

"Baby, you're practically geriatric. If I didn't know you, I'd swear you were nearing thirty!"

I nodded with satisfaction. The length of my long brown hair was pulled back in a tight ponytail to highlight the ten pounds of makeup I'd spackled on, and I wore a black syn-leather brassiere top with matching skirt. It was nice to be out of my conservative school uniform and in something sexy.

"What about me?" Shanel asked, skimming her palms over her curves.

I gave her a once-over. Moonlight seeped from the car windows and surrounded her in golden light. Her skin was pale and freckled, her eyes just a bit too large. She wore a tight pink dress that totally clashed with her mass of red curls, but somehow looked great on her. "Silver's going to be drooling over you."

Squealing, she clapped and held out her arm, wrist up. "Sweet. Now, smell me."

I sniffed and my nose wrinkled. "Uh, I'm sorry to tell you this, but you smell like dirt."

"Don't be sorry. That's wonderful news! I did a little recon and learned Morevvs adore earthy scents. I rubbed mud into all my pulse points just before I picked you up."

"Diabolical." I grinned.

The buildings outside were getting taller and closer together, so I knew we'd reach the club very soon. Another wave of nervousness hit me. "What if we can't get in?"

"Oh, will you stop worrying?" She ran her tongue over

her lips. "You know the Ell Rollis my dad hired to work on our house? Well, I commanded him to meet us at the club. He'll get us in."

My eyes widened. Ell Rollises were a race of ugly . . . things that smelled like garbage. They were big, unnaturally strong, and once given an order they thought only of that order. Only when the task was completed did they relax. If Shanel had ordered him to get us inside the Ship, he'd get us inside by any means necessary.

Maybe Erik would ask me to dance.

The car eased to a stop and a feminine computerized voice said, "Destination arrived."

Shanel uttered another squeal of delight and punched in the code for parking. A few seconds later, the car stopped. "This is going to be the greatest night of our lives!"

A girl could hope at least. We emerged and stood outside, gazing over at the club as a warm breeze slinked around us. Made of polished silver chrome, the Ship was shaped like a round, multilayered craft with hundreds of lights circling every other tier.

Even from this distance we could hear the gyrating music, a bump, bump, grind that demanded movement. A line stretched around the building and led all the way to the opening. I searched the masses for Erik, but I didn't see any sign of his (hot) body or (sexy) blond head. Was he already inside?

"You ready?" Shanel asked me.

Breathing deeply of perfumes, sweat, and eco-friendly exhaust, I gripped Shanel's hand. "Don't leave my side, okay?"

"Don't insult me. As if I'd leave you." She glanced toward the crowd and gasped happily. "Look. There's the Ell Rollis. Come on." She leapt into motion—leaving me behind.

With a sigh, I raced after her, high heels clicking against the pavement.

The closer we came to the club, the louder the music and voices became and the more realization set in. God, I could get in so much trouble for this. I usually obeyed my parents and followed their rules exactly. Only the thought of spending time with Erik had been able to lure me to the dark side.

Shanel ground to a stop in front of the male Ell Rollis who stood at the curb. When the Outer spotted her, he nodded in greeting. He had dry, yellow skin, no nose (that I could see), and sharp lizardlike teeth. I tried not to stare.

"I wait here just like you say," he told her, his voice heavily accented.

"Thank you, John. Now, here's what I want you to do next. Create a distraction so that Camille and I can get inside that building." She pointed to the double doors. "Then, run away and hide. Okay?"

John—what a weird name for such an inhuman creature—gave another nod and stomped in the direction Shanel had pointed, pushing through the thick crowd. We followed.

A few people gasped, a few growled in anger. Most smiled nervously and moved out of the way, as if their greatest wish was to please the hulking beast.

Up front, John skidded to a stop. Two burly guards waited behind a glowing, blue laserband that stretched across the doors, preventing anyone from passing. In unison, the men crossed their hands over their massive chests.

"I will distract you now," John told them.

The two men looked at each other and laughed.

"You're ugly and you stink," one said. "Go away."

Without another word, John reached out and grabbed him by the throat, lifting him off the ground. Murmurs and gasps swept through the crowd. Scared, I backed up a step. I might have even run back to the car, but Shanel tugged me into a shadowy corner.

"Let him go, you alien scum." The guard still standing withdrew a pyre-gun from his waist and aimed it at John's chest.

Before he could fire, John knocked it against the wall and it shattered. All the while, he shook the guy he held, the man's legs nearly touching the laserband. If they did, his clothes and skin would be horribly singed.

"Turn off the laser, Turk," he commanded his friend. His features were pale—no, blue. And only getting bluer. "Turn. Off. Laser."

I gulped.

"Laser!"

With a shaky hand, Turk punched in the code. Instantly the laser faded as if it had never been there.

John grinned and dropped the now-wheezing guard. "You good boys."

Shanel jerked me past the distracted pair, past the double doors, and into the building. Just like that, we were in. I glanced backward and watched as the crowd surged forward to get inside, as well. John headed in the opposite direction, sprinting away just as he'd been ordered.

Maybe *my* parents needed to employ an Ell Rollis. But they were expensive to keep, their appetites legendary, and more and more they were being picked up and locked away by the deadly and much-feared A.I.R. because too many humans commanded them to do bad things.

Who cares about that? You're in. In!

Shanel stopped, turned toward me, and wrapped me in a hug. "Can you believe it?" she shouted happily.

I grinned, all my worries melting away. The night, it seemed, had only just begun.

your attitude. **your style.**

MTV Books: totally your type.

Such a Pretty Girl
Laura Wiess

They promised
Meredith nine
years of safety,
but only gave her
three. She thought
she had time to
grow up, get out,
and start a new
life. But Meredith
is only fifteen, and
today, her father is
coming home from
prison. Today, her
time has run out.

A FAST GIRLS, HOT BOYS Novel

Beautiful Disaster
Kylie Adams

*Live fast....Die
young...Stay
pretty.* Senior year
is cooling down,
student scandals
are heating up,
and in sexy
South Beach, the
last killer party
becomes exactly
that—a party
that kills.

A BARD ACADEMY Novel

The Scarlet Letterman
Cara Lockwood

*Bad things happen
when fact and
fiction collide...*
Miranda Tate and
her closest friends
have been let in on
a powerful secret:
their teachers
are famous dead
writers.

www.simonsays.com/mtvbooks.com

BOOKS
Published by Pocket Books
A Division of Simon & Schuster
A CBS COMPANY